USA TODAY BESTSELLING AUTHOR

NIKKI LANDIS

Table of Contents

AUTHOR'S NOTE

Rattlin' Bones is the story of Marine veteran Michael Brandon "Skeletor" Myers, the new V.P for the Las Vegas, NV chapter of the Royal Bastards MC. As with all my books, please heed the CWs. This is a dark, motorcycle club romance with outlaws, revenge, violence, and biker slang.

Maddog and his shadow warriors are only getting started. Watch for more books in the Las Vegas, NV chapter. You can read *Claimed by the Bikers, One Night with the Bikers*, and *Twisted Iron*, which are all crossover stories with the RBMC.

Don't forget to catch up with the Reapers in the Tonopah, NV chapter of the Royal Bastards. Grim and his club hold a dark secret. Have you read about it yet?

If you love crossover stories, check out the Devil's Murder MC. The Tonopah Royal Bastards are close allies. The series begins with *Crow*.

ROYAL BASTARDS CODE

PROTECT: The club and your brothers come before anything else, and must be protected at all costs. **CLUB** is **FAMILY.**

RESPECT: Earn it & Give it. Respect club law. Respect the patch. Respect your brothers. Disrespect a member and there will be hell to pay.

HONOR: Being patched in is an honor, not a right. Your colors are sacred, not to be left alone, and **NEVER** let them touch the ground.

OL' LADIES: Never disrespect a member's or brother's Ol' Lady. **PERIOD.**

CHURCH is **MANDATORY.**

LOYALTY: Takes precedence over all, including well-being.

HONESTY: Never **LIE, CHEAT,** or **STEAL** from another member or the club.

TERRITORY: You are to respect your brother's property and follow their Chapter's club rules.

TRUST: Years to earn it...seconds to lose it.

NEVER RIDE OFF: Brothers do not abandon their family.

COMMON TERMS

RBMC Royal Bastards Motorcycle Club. One-percenter outlaw MC. Founded in Tonopah, NV 1985. Founded in Las Vegas, NV 2023.

Devil's Ride A deadly motorcycle ride into the Nevada desert and initiation into the club.

Shadow Rider/Warrior Spiritual entity that forms from shadow. Shares the body of every Royal Bastard club member in the Las Vegas chapter.

Reaper Demonic entity sharing the body of every Royal Bastard club member in the Tonopah chapter. A collector of souls at time of death.

Crossroads Bar & clubhouse owned by the RBMC Tonopah, NV chapter.

Pres President of the club. His word is law.

Brotherhood Unbreakable bond/kinship that transcends all other interpersonal relationships.

One-percenter Outlaw biker/club.

Ol' lady A member's woman, protected wife status.

Cut Leather vest worn by club members, adorned with patches and club colors, sacred to members.

Reaping Slang, killing those marked for death.

Church An official club meeting, led by president.

Chapel The location for church meetings in the clubhouse.

Prospect Probationary member sponsored by a ranking officer, banned from church until a full patch.

Full Patch A new member approved for membership.

Hog Motorcycle

Cage Vehicle

Muffler bunny Club girl, also called sweet butt, cut slut.

Bloody Scorpions MC Rival club to the Tonopah chapter.

Bladed Serpents MC Rival club to the Las Vegas chapter.

Businesses:

Tonopah –
Reaper's Custom Rides & Repairs
Grim Towing, LLC
Linked
Hope's Refuge
Millie's Diner

Las Vegas –
Maddog Bail & Recovery, LLC
Shadow Investigative Solutions

Rattlin'
BONES

Fear what hides in the shadows ...

Skel:

It's supposed to be a simple job—a request from my new president to scout a potential business.

The strip club in Vegas is nothing special, as routine as any other in the City of Sin. But when I walk in the door, I find a curvy blonde fighting off an overeager, handsy customer.

I step in, sweeping her into my arms and issuing a warning to anyone trying to force themselves on a woman. Lacey isn't grateful. She's pissed.

When I leave, I can't stop thinking about her. She intrigues me. It only takes a few seconds to realize she's just the type of woman I would fall for. Lacey is heaven on the eyes and hell on the heart.

She's wrong in every way: too young, troubled, on the opposite side of the law, and hiding a secret that could shatter the new club I joined.

I should stay away.

But I can't. I have to follow her home, ensuring she's safe. Something isn't right when I park my bike. Busting down her door, I stop a vicious attack, saving Lacey's life. Her enemy? It's the same one my club has declared war against.

Now, Lacey is mine to protect, and I won't let anyone harm her. She's got secrets, but I do, too.

It's almost Halloween. All the spooky, creepy things that play on the devil's night? I command them.

She has no idea how vicious I'll become to end every threat against her and the club. I'm unleashing the monster within, and he's got a ravenous appetite.

Rattlin' Bones is part of the **Royal Bastards MC** world. It's a dark romance with a Halloween theme, violence, biker slang, steamy scenes, torture, revenge, and a slight paranormal twist. One woman's quest to stop injustice becomes a veteran's redemption. This wicked tale features a possessive, protective, outlaw V.P., and the determined woman who'll risk her life to ensure a criminal faces the judge for his crimes.

ROYAL BASTARDS MC

Chapter 1

LACEY

THREE YEARS EARLIER

Cool wind brushed across my bare shoulders as I stared up at the orange, heavily rounded sphere of a harvest moon. I couldn't remember the last time I paused to notice how the craters and shadows played hide and seek over the surface or how the clouds rolled by like endless waves of smoky gray in a turbulent sea.

Behind the moon, a reddish hue served as a bold outline that faded into the darkness and spread beyond its bubble shape in an eerily prophetic declaration of impending death. The warmth of the color didn't extend below the horizon or offer any heat despite its encroaching position on the rows of graves spreading across the cemetery.

A chill slowly climbed over my chest and settled, squatting on my lungs and squeezing until I began to panic, sucking in air, violently gasping as it felt like I tried to pull oxygen through a dozen tiny straws. The ache burned through my sternum.

1

Shit. My asthma. What a rotten time to flare up.

My body sent urgent, desperate messages to my brain, but it didn't matter. I still couldn't breathe. My mouth opened and closed, the attempt feeble. Clawing my right hand to the side, I dug through the dry, scratchy blades of grass beneath my fingertips, slowly managing to angle my body as I reached toward the pocket of my hoodie. My only salvation rested in a plastic holder that held my inhaler.

This whole process would be a hell of a lot simpler if I weren't tied up. With my wrists and ankles bound, I would remain by these headstones until someone stumbled upon me or the ghosts that lingered in this old cemetery decided to kick me out. The position was awkward enough, but the extra piece of rope connecting my wrists to my ankles didn't have enough slack to allow for much movement.

Fumbling with the inhaler case, I felt it slip through my hand and drop to the ground. As I reached for it, I bumped the edge with my knuckle and knocked it out of reach. *Well, fuck.*

Ever have one of those days? The kind of day that was a cluster of errors, mistakes, and rotten luck. Where nothing went right, and you just wanted to climb back into bed and forget every minute. I had that day today. All because I was in the wrong place at the wrong time.

I tried to cough and wheezed, lowering my head to the rough surface of the nearest headstone. My mouth gaped like a fish out of water, and I thought I heard something rumbling on the ground beneath my ear. Multiple Vehicles? Or was it just my imagination and thunder? I didn't know.

Bright light flashed in my eyes as I groaned. I turned my head away from the steady glare of white and scooted my bottom, hoping to hide from whoever headed in my direction. My chest felt so tight I thought it would cave in, desperate enough for air to crack wide open in hopes of being able to function again. My vision tunneled as spots flickered in my peripheral.

In just a few more seconds, I would probably pass out.

"Shit! You okay?"

I attempted to answer but couldn't.

"Who the fuck tied you up and left you out here?"

The deep voice sounded pissed.

"Inhaler," I managed to croak.

"I got it," the stranger answered, rushing to grab the medicine, shaking it a couple of times before he placed the plastic end against my lips.

He knew what to do. I inhaled two puffs and immediately felt my lungs begin to cooperate, opening up to allow me to breathe easier.

"This is fucked," I heard the guy mutter.

I still couldn't see him well. The blinding light kept him hidden in shadow. Blinking, I stared at his face, barely making out a strong jawline and rugged features, lifting my hands. Something seemed odd, but I dismissed it. "Could you help take these off?"

"Goddamn zip ties? Who the hell did you piss off?"

I didn't do a damn thing. The problem was my bloodline.

"Hold still. I don't want to cut you."

I didn't move as I felt him cut through the hard nylon and it snapped. "Not me. My dad," I clarified as I groaned, and the restraints dropped from my wrists. "I'm nothing but a casualty of war."

"What war?"

"The law and criminals."

He snorted. "Not sure what that means, Darlin'."

"My dad is a judge."

"What's his name?"

I probably shouldn't have been so trusting. I had already landed in a cemetery close to midnight, and who knew what else Luis Diego had planned. What if he came back?

"Maxwell."

"Judge Curtis Maxwell?"

So he heard of my father. "That's the one."

"He's got a rep. Tough on crime. Even tougher on repeat offenders."

"I guess so." I shrugged. "He wants to clean up Las Vegas."

A dark chuckle followed my words. "City of Sin ain't ever gonna change. It's corrupt to the core. Sex. Drugs. Crime. People love it because anything is possible."

"That's also why they fear it."

He reached for my hands and helped me to my feet. "You're too observant, Sweet Girl. From what I gather, the sharks are already circling, and you're blood in the water."

A weird analogy. "I can't help who I'm related to."

"No, but you can play it smart and stay outta trouble." He shifted his stance and turned to the side, shielding my eyes from the light.

I immediately noticed two things. One, the bright beam had come from the headlight on a big Harley Davidson. Two, the guy stood about half a foot taller than me. On his face, he wore a mask. Funny, but I didn't notice that his voice had been muffled. It must have been loose enough to allow him to breathe and speak without interference.

The mask, though. . . it spooked the hell out of me: a macabre grin and a bony, sinister stare. I backed up, but he followed, keeping pace until I nearly fell over a headstone.

His hands shot out and gripped my waist, keeping me from falling on my ass. "Name's Skeletor. Skel, for short. You should know it."

Shit. "Why?" I was almost afraid to ask.

"Because I'm invested in your safety now."

Invested? "What does that mean?"

"It's not every day that I find a pretty girl all trussed up and sittin' on my grandaddy's grave. My mother is buried beside him. I figure our meetin' isn't chance. It's fate."

I pursed my lips. "You're crazy, Skel." I couldn't help the small laugh that escaped. "But I do owe you. You saved me from frost, bugs, and probably from wetting my pants. Thank you."

The mask lifted around his chin; I guessed he must have smiled at that.

"You're bleedin'," he announced as he turned over my wrists.

The zip ties had cut into my skin. "It's not that painful."

"We should get you cleaned up."

"I suppose so." With a sigh, I wondered how long I had sat on the cold ground with the wind whipping through the trees and over my exposed skin. I had worn a lightweight hoodie but still had on jean shorts. At least I wore socks and athletic shoes.

"I feel a little lightheaded," I admitted, falling into him as I took a step and stumbled. My balance was off. I hadn't lost much blood, so I couldn't think of a reason for it. Dehydration? Maybe.

"How long have you been out here?"

My cheek rested over the black long-sleeved tee he wore. The soft material had grown warm from his body heat, and I snuggled into him, realizing I was freezing. "I don't know. What time is it?"

"Almost four a.m."

"What? Really?" I lifted my head and caught his nod. "I think they dumped me here around 11."

"Who?"

"Luis Diego and a few men I didn't recognize."

"Fuck," Skel growled. "I'm gettin' you outta here, warm and cleaned up. Then you're gonna tell me everything."

5

His tone didn't allow any room for argument. Truth be told, I didn't have the energy. If I wasn't ready to pass out from this ordeal, I probably would have argued. My father once told me I should change majors in college and become a lawyer. I guessed I had the skills for it.

"Where are we going?" I asked instead of refusing his help.

"My place. It isn't far."

"Okay." I needed to contact my dad and hoped it wouldn't be a problem. He was probably sick with worry. I never stayed out this late without checking in. It wasn't because he loved rules but because he loved me and worried about my safety with his judicial position.

Skel slipped an arm around my waist and led me toward his bike. "You ever ride before?"

Yeah. A few times. "Sure. My ex had a bike."

He snorted. "A Harley?"

"Well, no," I admitted.

"Then it wasn't a bike, Sweet Girl." Skel held onto me until I sat on his seat, then opened his saddlebags and pulled out a sweatshirt. "It's gonna get cold, and you're not wearin' enough clothes. This will help."

I nodded as he slipped it over my head, and I shoved my arms through the sleeves, noting that it was so large that it fell over my thighs and covered me even with the hoodie I had on. "Thanks."

"Yeah, I don't want you to fall off from all that shivering."

I didn't expect the teasing tone he used. "I'll just have to snuggle you."

He threw a leg over his seat and joined me. "Hold on tight."

I planned on it. My arms slid around his torso, and I clenched them, wincing as I remembered the cuts. Ouch.

"Here, let me help." Skel pulled the material of his sweatshirt over my hands as I clasped them. "That wind is gonna hurt. It'll be brutally cold once we pick up speed."

"But we're not going far, right?"

"Yeah. Stay tough, Baby."

Baby? I never had a chance to reply.

Skel's motorcycle rumbled as he started it, the vibrations beneath us both exciting and terrifying. I knew better than to trust strangers or agree to go home with a guy I met the same night. But this was different. Skel rescued me.

He wouldn't hurt me. If he tried, I had pepper spray in my front pocket. I managed to sneak it before Luis confiscated my purse and phone. I never had a chance to use it with my bound wrists, but if Skel turned out to be a creep, I wouldn't hesitate.

Feeling better with a plan, I huddled into his warmth as the bike picked up speed, turned onto the road, and headed away from the Strip's bright neon lights. The cemetery was just off Las Vegas Boulevard. Skel reached for my hands as we pulled to a stop, idling at a red light, and I wondered if he was checking my grip.

"Still too cold," he announced in a low, raspy tone, giving my fingers a squeeze.

When the light turned green, we shot forward, moving farther from the end of town where I lived with my dad. We had a penthouse in one of the most expensive high-rises in Vegas. Since I attended UNLV, I didn't bother with my own place. Plus, it worried my dad when I spent too much time on campus or in the dorms.

As we road into Skel's neighborhood, I didn't know what I expected, but it wasn't the quiet street Skel turned down, or the sprawling ranch-style house with a two-car garage that he declared was his property. The open layout and large windows were casual and inviting.

Skel clicked a garage door opener, and we rolled to a stop inside before he shut off the engine. I stood on shaky legs as my gaze traveled to the driveway and the barren street.

"You could run if you want, but I wouldn't advise it. I'd only chase you down and bring you back. You're in no condition to wander off alone."

He was right.

"And it's not safe," he added.

I knew that. "I want to call my father and let him know I'm okay."

"You give me thirty minutes to get you settled, and I'll hand over my cell."

"Deal," I agreed.

As the garage door began to close, I followed Skel inside his house, wondering what kind of man wore a mask and rescued a kidnapped, injured woman abandoned in a cemetery in the middle of the night.

It occurred to me that he said he was visiting a grave. A family member, if I recall correctly. Well, shit. I had something in common with my masked savior.

We both lost a parent, specifically our mother.

"Come on, Sweet Girl. I don't bite."

The door shut behind me with a click as I stepped inside, curious about the man behind the mask and hoping he planned to remove it.

ROYAL BASTARDS MC

Chapter 2

SKEL

PRESENT

"WHERE THE HELL ARE you, man?" Maddog growled as I swiped across my cell to answer his call. "We got shit to discuss in church."

"I'll be there."

"When?"

"Soon."

He snorted. "What are you doin'? Stalking that blonde again?"

Maybe. "Something ain't sittin' right."

"Tell me you're not late for church because of pussy."

"Pres," I began, knowing he wouldn't understand. It was Lacey. If there were any woman I'd risk Maddog's wrath for, it was her.

"For fuck's sake, Skel. Get your ass here. Now."

9

He hung up.

Shit.

Like the bastard I was, I dialed him back, not giving him a chance to talk as he answered. "Flint, this is important. I need to talk to Lacey."

"So is church," he growled.

"It is. Just got to handle this first."

"Creature is countin' on you. Don't keep us waitin'."

"I won't," I relented. This wasn't about getting my dick wet. I had other reasons for needing to see Lacey.

"Good. Be here by noon."

When he hung up the second time, I knew I had to make this quick. My bike idled across the street from the ritzy high-rise building where Lacey lived with her father. She'd stayed there through college graduation and never moved out.

How did I know? Easy. I stalked, uh kept tabs, on her.

I shut down the engine and approached the entrance, slipping inside when a couple exited and left the door open wide. There was a doorman and a guard on duty, so the security wasn't awful, but there were too many goddamn windows. I knew from experience how easy it could be to watch someone and learn their routine. The elevators were easy to access, but the penthouse? It had its own elevator down the hall, partially hidden by a plant with obscenely large fronds.

James, the doorman, greeted me as I entered. "You've come for another visit, Mr. Myers?"

Yeah, he remembered me. I didn't know if that was good or bad. I guess I was about to find out.

"Yeah," I answered. "What's it been? Three years?"

I knew exactly how long it had been since I last walked inside this building instead of entering through a disguise.

"I believe so. Is Ms. Lacey expecting you?"

No. Well, maybe. "She should be," I replied, walking to the penthouse elevator and pressing the button.

"I'll just give her a little ring to be sure."

Oh, he remembered me. Didn't like me much either. It probably had a lot to do with the cut on my back, the heavy ink on my skin, and the fact that I didn't bow to any man, law or not.

Appearance was everything when you moved within the circle of the elite. Rich, beautiful, and powerful people surrounded themselves with the same cookie-cutter types. Didn't bother me except for the fact that they judged everyone else. Like James, who didn't have a horse in this race but felt he needed to add his opinion anyhow.

He should be thankful considering I helped him out last time we met.

"You do that," I hollered back, not bothering to hide my irritation as I mashed the button, waiting for the doors to open. Once they did, I entered, leaning against the smudge-free wall of the interior, noting that not even a fingerprint marred its perfect appearance.

How the fuck did people live like this?

Privilege, that's how—spoiled and pampered from birth.

Like Lacey. Only she was different.

When the doors opened, I stepped onto the black marble floor and noted the luxuriant décor. The opulent hall with crystal chandeliers and gold accents led straight to Lacey's door. There wasn't a need to knock. She stood in the doorway.

"Why have you come back?"

Her attitude wasn't lost on me. She had every reason not to trust me and think the worst. I didn't give her much choice after what I did.

"For you," I answered simply.

She lifted her chin. "I don't think so."

I wondered what lies her daddy had spun to turn her against me. It didn't matter. That wasn't the reason I came.

"Luis Diego is back in Vegas," I revealed. "You need protection."

She scoffed. "And you're offering your services?"

I never stopped. She might have thought so, but I made a point of keeping tabs on her and Diego. There wasn't a reason to intervene until Diego ignored my warning and returned, placing Lacey in danger.

"I'll never allow him to harm you again."

Her expression faltered before she lifted her chin. "That was a long time ago. You don't owe me anything."

No, I didn't. That wasn't the point. "Gotta be sure he doesn't try to finish the job he started."

Lacey sighed. "I don't need your help, Skel. You made it clear when you left Vegas and said you weren't coming back."

I fucked up. Sue me. I wasn't fucking perfect. "Never planned on it, Sweet Girl. When Luis Diego got out of prison and went back on his promise, I had to intervene."

"That doesn't mean you had to come *here*," she pointed out.

"I needed to see you." I closed the distance between us, caging her against the doorjamb. "Things got fucked up, Baby. I shouldn't have left the way I did."

She frowned. "Was it my father? Did he pay you?"

Fuck no. How goddamn insulting. "No," I growled. "No one pays me off for shit."

I didn't expect the sudden tears she blinked back. "Then why did you go?"

Fuck. "I had to."

"I'm still waiting for the reason, not to mention an apology."

Apology? "For what?"

"Breaking my heart," she whispered before shoving me away and closing the door in my fucking face.

Fuck! I had to make this right.

Spinning on my heel, I stomped to the elevators. Lacey didn't understand. I wasn't going anywhere.

"WHAT DID YOU FIND, Skel?" Maddog asked as we gathered around the table in church, as serious as a sermon on the Sabbath. No, we didn't pray to any higher being, but we were just as strict and uncompromising about our beliefs. We lived by a code of brotherhood and loyalty, and the club took first place over every other relationship each member had. Only family trumped that and the few ol' ladies claimed by officers.

But that wasn't the focus of this meeting today.

"I did a deep dive on the web," I reminded them, continuing the conversation we'd had last week. "I found information about a hit ordered by the Bladed Serpents." They were our biggest rival. "It was issued when Creature's father was V.P."

Creature pounded a fist on the table. "I need to know more about how his own club called a hit on my family. Those motherfuckers plotted to kill my mother."

Creature's mother was murdered right in front of him when he was only thirteen. Fucked him up good. Back then, I had been a prospect for the Bladed Serpents. Young and stupid, I didn't know the shit they were involved in or how deep the animosity ran toward Tinman. That day changed everything.

I swore I'd never put a patch on my back unless it was with men I could respect and trust.

Now, over a decade later, there were still secrets. Creature took out Mateo Ruiz, but his business associates, Luis Diego, and Angel Mackenzie, were still out there, causing chaos. They had a deal with the Bladed Serpents and Ratchet, their president, who trafficked women in and out of the U.S. at various checkpoints, including Las Vegas.

He needed put down, preferably six feet deep. The Feral Rebels MC, a brother chapter to ours and the Tonopah RBMC, had already declared war on the Bladed Serpents. We were the next to add our vote.

"Ratchet was the treasurer when Tinman was V.P.," Creature reminded us. "If he didn't order the hit on my mother, he has to know something about it."

"I've found some shady shit with the club's books online," I divulged. "There's a connection that's mentioned multiple times. Luis Diego. But someone isn't as good with accounting as they think. If they get audited, shit will go down with the feds."

"We should look into making that happen," Creature decided. He turned to Maddog. "Pres?"

"Yeah, that's the first angle we dig around. Do it," Maddog ordered.

I was the best tech person we had until Snapshot joined us. He wouldn't arrive for another month. It was up to me to help put pressure on Ratchet and the Bladed Serpents. Maybe that would draw out Luis, too. I had a bullet with his name on it. The cocksucker. He messed with the RBMC, the Feral Rebels, and Lacey. He was fucking done.

I thought I saw the last of him three years ago, but he was out of prison early. Probably starting shit. I'd handle it.

Our enemies were growing bold and plotting against us. Ratchet. Luis Diego. And fucking Angel Mackenzie, the nephew of cartel boss Salazar Guerrero. Salazar failed to control his nephew. That meant Angel was fair game now. They were all connected and about to face judgment.

Creature cleared his throat. "After all this time, I'm finally gonna find the motherfucker who ordered my mother's murder. There's not gonna be any mercy once I do, pres."

"Wouldn't think otherwise," Maddog replied, lifting the gavel and slamming it down on the table. "Church is dismissed."

Manic and Creature left the chapel as I lit up a smoke. "What are you thinkin'?"

"Can't ever keep shit from you, can I?" he asked with a laugh.

"No," I agreed. "Tell me what's on your mind."

"I need an honest opinion on the strip club we just purchased. Something is up. I bought out the old management, but they're still hanging around the place. Need you to figure out why."

That was odd. "The girls? Money? Or you think illegal shit is goin' down?"

"It's Vegas," he deadpanned.

Right. "We'll go with illegal."

A dark chuckle followed. "I got a weird feelin' in my gut. I hate that shit. You goin' in means no one checkin' out the club has seen you yet. You've not been here long. It works to our advantage. You can pretend to be a payin' customer."

"Pretend?" I laughed.

"Fine. Get a lap dance or a blowie. I don't give a fuck. Just find out what the hell is goin' down there. Bouncers aren't sayin' shit. I need to hire new staff."

"Yeah, you do. We'll get to that once I scope the place out."

"I was hopin' you'd say that, Skelly."

Fuck. I hated that nickname. "Flint," I warned.

His laughter lasted a full minute. "Just fuckin' with you, man. Ain't seen you in months."

"I know." I cleared my throat, curbing my irritation. "I'll handle this, Maddog."

"That's why I'm sendin' you. You're my new V.P. No one else I want by my side half as much."

"You sappy old fuck," I joked, steering the emotional aspect of the conversation as far as possible. I didn't do feelings. Too goddamn messy. And they always skewed the focus and mission. *Especially with Lacey.*

He snorted. "We'll make it official tomorrow. Gonna take you for a ride into the desert."

The desert? "That sounds sketchy."

"You have no idea. Check-in with me when you know somethin'. I'll be up late."

"You got it."

Maddog stood, leaving me alone in the chapel as he moved toward the bar and hollered for a drink. I finished the cigarette, flicked the butt into an ashtray, and headed toward the exit—time to get movin'.

Outside, I sat on my Harley, starting the engine as I pulled out my phone and checked the display for messages. One from my pops. A few social media notifications. Nothing from Lacey.

I didn't expect her to contact me. Didn't think she'd be in a rush to rehash any arguments we already had. That was why I had a tracker on her phone. In three years, she'd never noticed it. Win for me.

Lacey's location pinged close to the clubhouse. With a frown, I looked closer at the app. *Motherfucker.*

My stubborn, reckless woman was only a few doors down from my location. The exact spot? A strip club, specifically the one I planned to visit. Why the fuck was she there?

I planned to find out. Now.

Riding toward the location, instead of walking in case I needed to drag Lacey out and leave in a hurry, I left the clubhouse parking lot. One of our new prospects opened the gate, saluting as I rode by. I shook my head. I'd have to fix that.

16

When Maddog first called and asked me to join his new club, a brother chapter for the Royal Bastards MC, I leaped at the chance to leave California.

Life was stagnant. I couldn't seem to date anyone without comparing every woman I knew to Lacey. She invaded my mind and my heart three years ago and everything since had been shit. It didn't matter that I caused the separation. I thought I was doing the right thing. Turned out I had nothin' but regret now.

After two failed relationships, several jobs that never lasted long, and my restless need to find purpose, I was ready for something new. That was the thing no one ever told you about once you left active duty in the Marine Corps, how life would never seem as exciting, dangerous, or busy after sacrificing for the government.

Once a Marine, always a Marine. You retired or chose not to reenlist, but there was no "former" title. That life and its strict, rigorous structure stayed with you long after you stopped wearing your cammies.

I reached my destination and parked close to the entrance with plenty of light so no brave motherfucker might try to fuck with my bike. I invested in a high-quality cam last year, and I'd hunt down anyone stupid enough to fuck with my Harley.

Everything in Vegas was flashy, and this strip club was no different. The neon sign above the entrance blinked with a bare limb and included a red high heel. Below it, another sign read TOPLESS in all caps. You couldn't miss it.

Loud music pumped through speakers placed around the room as I entered, pausing to take in the scene. A pole had been erected in the center, and two women wearing nothin' but thongs danced in front of a large crowd. There were three stages, all with poles, and every one of them had a dancer wrapped around it.

Good business. I could see this place turned a hefty profit. With a little work and a remodel, this club could bring in major cash flow.

Tables mainly were full, and several long couches with red leather lined the perimeter on either side of the bar. A few male patrons were receiving lap dances while nearly every stool was occupied. Men laughed and drank, interacting with the topless waitresses who served drinks and cozied up for extra tips. I noted the two bartenders were a redhead and a blonde. Both were smokin' hot and flashed broad smiles.

The management had taken time to train their talent. I could appreciate that. The girls were good lookin' and not afraid to flirt. I liked the dancers knew how to work a pole. None of them hesitated to throw themselves into it, flinging their bodies around as tits and asses shook all over the damn club.

The décor could use updated. My gaze swept over the room, and I could see old stains and dirt that hadn't been cleaned regularly. That would be one of the first things I changed. Sure, they wiped the tables and cleaned the poles. Probably the bar, too. But I wasn't sure the floors, walls, and seats got the same treatment. Considering all the fluids that could drip around here, I wasn't taking chances on what could spread.

The old management must have cared more about money and talent than sanitation, but they all fit together. All three were needed to run a successful business, especially long term. I'd have to bring it up to Maddog as I made a mental list of the other things I needed to add.

There were doors that led to private rooms, and it was obvious some of those lap dance offers included personal time with the girls for the right fee. Selling sex wasn't new to Vegas, but it was still illegal. If the club wanted to run this business and turn a profit, we'd have to restrict sexual activity. The girls could do what they wanted on their own time.

I headed toward the bar, taking a seat on an empty stool. I didn't see Lacey yet and hoped the tracker was wrong.

"Hey, handsome. What can I get for you?" The redhead bartender beamed a wide smile and leaned over the bar, pushing her tits closer as she regarded me. "Never saw you around here before. I'd remember."

"Just got in town," I revealed. "Need a beer, Darlin'.'"

"You got it." She winked. "I'm Maris. Need anything besides alcohol, I'm your girl."

"What about them?" I ticked my head toward the dancers.

"That's just fourplay."

Damn. She was layin' it on thick. "Just the beer," I answered, uninterested in Maris and her enticing offer.

A different woman took up all the available space in my head and kept me up at night. A feisty, curvy goddess that had stolen my heart the night we met. In a graveyard, no less.

And that was when I saw my sweet girl, my sexy as fuck blonde with hair down to her juicy ass and smooth, tanned skin spent from plenty of hours in the hot Nevada sunshine. Long bare legs snared my attention, and I slowly dragged my gaze upward, pausing to appreciate her generous tits before landing on her face. *You'll be coming home with me.*

Concerned about the reason she was serving drinks in this fucking strip club, I chugged my beer. The bottle hit the bar as I pushed away, stalking my way toward my prize. I'd know her sultry smile, luscious ass, and pretty blue eyes anywhere. She looked different with all the makeup and skimpy clothes. A wilder version of my sexy, doe-eyed vixen. She was goddamn beautiful. Almost took my breath away, the same as she did the night we met.

I'm back, baby. This time, I'm making sure you're mine.

I didn't get more than a few steps when one of the customers got handsy. He reached for her ass and slapped it. Before I could react, Lacey pushed him away, trying to escape as he slid off a stool and grabbed her around the waist.

No one touched Lacey. NO. ONE.

I shoved the guy out of the way as I reached him, swinging at the same time. My fist connected with his jaw and sent his drunk ass sprawling across the floor. I glared down at him, daring this asshole to fight me.

"Get the fuck away from her. Now."

ROYAL BASTARDS MC

Chapter 3

LACEY

THREE YEARS EARLIER

"THE BATHROOM IS THIS way," Skel informed me, reaching for my hand to lead me in the right direction, although it wasn't hard to figure out with an open floor plan.

We walked through a spacious kitchen, cutting through the dining room to reach a hallway and the first door on the right. Skel entered and flipped on the light before he released my hand. He gestured to the sink, and I hopped up, facing him as he opened the cabinet and began digging around for supplies.

I waited while he wet a washcloth he snatched from a nearby shelf, pumping a dollop of soap onto the material before he held out his hand.

"It might sting while I wash your cuts."

I could have done it myself, but I allowed him to clean the wounds, growing more intrigued by him the longer I spent in his presence. "Thanks," I replied when he finished.

He kept the mask on. Inside under the lights, it made him less menacing and more mysterious. Every fantasy I ever had about masks and hot sex seemed to pop into my mind. Worst timing ever. The sexy stranger with his deep voice, bulging muscles, tattoos, and snug tee shirt reminded me of the taboo romance novels I liked to sneak and read late at night.

You know the ones. Smut. A little plot. Hot as fuck bad boy.

Get a grip, Lacey. Stop sexualizing your masked savior.

Bandages were placed over the raw skin on my wrists before he tidied up his mess. Impressed with his attention to detail, I smiled. "You're good at this."

"I live alone." He shrugged. "If I don't do it, no one is here to help."

True. But I knew plenty of people who procrastinated. He didn't seem like the type to be that way. He was so controlled. Precise. Careful in a way that made me wonder if he had training like the military. I bet he was skilled with his hands.

"You thirsty?"

His question made me focus instead of letting my imagination run wild.

"Yes. I need to use the facilities first," I admitted, noting my urgent bladder.

"Uh, right." He walked to the door, glancing my way before he shut it.

Yes, I locked it behind him. I couldn't help it. My bladder was full, and I didn't want to defend myself while seated on a toilet.

After I washed my hands, I opened the door, following the noises he was making back to the kitchen. He seemed to be intentionally clanging things together like he wanted me to know he wasn't waiting around the corner with a length of rope to tie me back up. I didn't think he would try anything after how nice he'd been, but I read that some serial killers lulled their victims into a false sense of security before they attacked. They liked the cat and mouse game.

Even if it was true, I felt safe with my rescuer, if you didn't count the creepy skeleton mask. "Are you going to take off the mask?" I asked as I joined him, taking a seat on one of his stools that faced his direction. The breakfast bar had enough room for four people and plenty of space to entertain. Interesting. Did he have friends or women over often?

"I suppose it's a bit odd to wear it inside."

Yes, it seemed weird to insist on it. My stomach fluttered in anticipation. Would he be handsome? Scarred?

He pulled up the mask, lifted it over his head, and tossed it onto the counter beside the stove. Damn it. He didn't turn around. I watched him stirring something in a pot. Since he was cooking, I couldn't see his face yet.

The wait was killing me. "What are you making?"

"Soup. Figured you could use the broth."

How thoughtful.

"I appreciate that."

"It's no trouble." He turned off the burner, poured the soup into a bowl, and brought it to me. He added a spoon and a hunk of warm bread as he placed it down.

I blinked. "You're full of surprises."

Soft, masculine laughter shook his chest. "Maybe."

When I glanced at his face, I nearly gasped. He wasn't at all what I expected. For one, he was much older than I first realized. I thought he'd been closer to my age, but I was wrong. Light scruff covered his square jaw. A mustache and goatee in a dark brown tinted with red stood out against his tanned skin. He had expressive hazel eyes and high cheekbones. His nose was straight and the perfect size, neither too big nor too small for his features.

His head was shaven, and the rugged look, handsome face, loads of dark ink, and towering height made him pure eye candy. At least for me.

"I thought you were my age," I blurted when I noticed I had been staring far too long without saying anything.

The corners of his eyes crinkled. "I'll be forty in a few years."

"I'm a little younger than that," I joked, not wanting to admit how many years spanned between us.

"If I had to guess, I'd say you're in your early twenties."

"Twenty-two," I admitted. "But I'm mature for my age."

He winked. "I'm sure you are."

This had gotten weird fast. I felt his stare as I finished my soup. With the bowl nearly empty, I pushed it away. My body felt stiff. I slid from the stool and nearly fell over.

Skel rushed to my side. "You're weak. I bet it's just fatigue."

He was probably right. "I need to get home." I stifled a yawn. "Could I use your phone now?"

"Sure." He handed it over, unlocking the screen as he led me to a couch. I sat down, feeling far too lightheaded. I was going to pass out soon. The food and warm atmosphere let my body relax and I'd gotten far too comfortable with Skel and his home.

I wasn't looking forward to this call. My father was going to lose his shit once he knew I was okay. Ever since my mom died, he worried about me like it was a second full-time job. He answered the number after only one ring, even though it wasn't someone he knew. "Dad?"

"Lacey! Where the hell have you been? I've been calling your phone for hours. Whose number is this?"

"I'm okay. I promise. It's a long story."

"Are you hurt? Do you need help?" He sounded frantic.

"Dad. I'm fine. A friend is bringing me home."

"What happened?"

"I think I should tell you in person."

He sucked in a breath. "Did some asshole force himself on you?"

"No. Not like you're implying."

"I don't like the sound of that, Lace."

"We'll talk about it once I'm home. I promise."

"How far away are you? I can pick you up or send Larry."

Larry was our driver. He chauffeured my dad everywhere.

"I've got a ride. See you soon. And Dad?"

"Yeah, honey?"

"I love you."

"Lacey, you're scaring me. Where are you?"

"Close. I'll see you in twenty minutes."

"I'm not moving from this door until I see you."

"Okay. Bye, Dad."

He grunted, not wanting to hang up. I ended the call.

"Thanks." I held out the cell, and Skel pocketed it.

"You ready, Lacey?"

I nodded but closed my eyes.

"Honey, you just called your father. If he doesn't see you in twenty minutes, he's gonna send out a search party."

I blinked as Skel sat beside me. "How did you know that?"

"It's what I would do."

That didn't surprise me at all.

"I'm really tired," I complained. "What if I close my eyes for just five minutes?"

"No, Sweet Girl. We need to leave. And I don't think it's safe for you to ride my bike. I've got a truck. We'll use that. Come on."

I didn't move.

"Lacey." He shook his head. "I'll carry you then."

I didn't protest as he picked me up, scooping under my legs. My head rested on his shoulder as I snuggled into his body. "You're nice and warm."

"It's a bit concerning how fast and easy you trust me," he murmured.

"I already saw evil tonight, Skel. I think I'd know if I ran across it again."

He squeezed me once and headed toward the garage. "That actually made sense."

WHEN WE ARRIVED AT my building, I was glad Skel wasn't wearing his mask. It would have freaked out my dad. Not to mention the motorcycle. Skel had pulled on his sweatshirt after I removed it as we parked by the entrance. His appearance wasn't near as intimidating now.

My father didn't exaggerate. He stood by the security guard and waited for me to enter the building, frowning at Skel. "Who the hell are you?"

"Her ride home," Skel answered, not intimidated by the judge.

"He's also the guy who saved me, Dad. Be nice." I walked into his open arms, hugging my father tight.

"Saved you from who?"

"The guys who kidnapped me." I already knew how this would sound to my dad and Skel. Judging by their twin scowls, I knew both men were concerned.

"You forgot to mention that part," Skel huffed, "but now I know why you were out in that cemetery."

My father gripped my shoulders as I stepped back. "And you're not hurt? They didn't do anything to you?"

I shook my head. "No. They tied me up and dropped me at the cemetery. I think it was a warning."

"Who did this?" Skel asked.

"Not here," I whispered, uncomfortable with the security guard and James listening in. I wanted to talk about this to my father without an audience.

"Let's go up." My dad guided me toward the elevator that led to our penthouse.

"Sir," Skel began. "I'd like to be a part of this conversation."

Dad raised an eyebrow, asking what I thought.

I nodded. "He might be able to help."

"What's your name?"

"Bran."

Bran? I thought it was Skel. How many names did he have?

"Well, Bran, I want to know more about how you helped my daughter. Join us."

It wasn't a question. More like an order.

Skel stepped onto the elevator, and the doors closed. When we arrived on our floor, Dad helped me down the hall, unlocking our door before stepping inside.

I moved to the couch, curling up with one of my favorite blankets. Several of the softest materials were kept in the ottoman. I snatched one out and covered up, resting my head against the back of the cushion. "I feel like I could sleep for weeks."

"Not until you tell me what happened," my father announced. "Who took you?" He sat on the edge of the couch, tensing as he awaited my answer.

"He said his name was Luis Diego. That you would know his name," I added. "He said you owe him a debt, and he'll come to collect if you don't follow through." I swallowed, terrified of what that meant.

"Fuck." Skel sat down beside me. "I don't think he's fucking around."

"I know that," my father spat. "I've been on the circuit for twenty years and sent more scumbags to prison than you could count. Luis Diego is just another criminal with a god complex. He thinks he can force my hand."

Force his hand? "What does that mean?" I already knew this had something to do with one of my father's cases. I just didn't know how dangerous Luis Diego was or if he'd make good on his threat.

"There's a murder trial on the docket for next week. I'm guessing he's asking me to be lenient since the defendant also shares the same last name."

Shit. "Dad. I think you should take this seriously."

"I already am." His sharp gaze focused on me. "The police are on the way to his residence now."

I paled. "Is there enough evidence to bring him in?"

My father clenched his phone hard enough for it to crack. "Luis kidnapped and threatened you. He threatened a judge. He won't be walking out of that jail anytime soon."

Relieved, I nodded. "Okay."

Skel didn't seem appeased by that answer. "I could help."

My father shot him a doubtful look. "I don't know who you are or why you helped my daughter. I'm thankful for your assistance, but your services are no longer needed."

I sighed. When my father got like this, reasoning with him was almost impossible. "How can you help, uh, Bran?"

Skel's lips twitched. He seemed pleased that I picked up on his real name, which meant Skel was an alias or nickname.

"I run a private investigation business. I'm good at finding secrets."

Wow. He was a P.I.? Interesting.

"I already have the best tech experts on the city payroll working on this case. They're digging into Juan Diego's financials and background. I've added Luis to the list after tonight."

"But it wouldn't hurt to have a P.I. helping us, right? What if he can find things your connections can't?" I asked, hoping to convince my father to hire Skel.

"Perhaps," Dad agreed. "Do you have a card?"

Skel reached into his pocket and pulled out his wallet. Reaching inside, he removed a card and presented it to my father. "Shadow Investigative Solutions. I'm currently taking on new clients." He glanced my way and winked.

"Consider yourself hired on a probationary basis. Provide something useful, and I'll hire you on a more permanent basis."

"I appreciate that, Judge Maxwell."

My eyes closed. Exhaustion left me weak and unable to stay awake. "Goodnight," I whispered, already drifting asleep.

"Night, Sweet Girl."

I heard him leave and wondered how long it would be before I saw Skel again.

ROYAL BASTARDS MC

Chapter 4

LACEY

PRESENT

"GET THE FUCK AWAY from her. Now," Skel rumbled, placing his body in front of mine.

God, that growl was sexy. Everything about Skel turned me on, and I hated it. He knew how he affected me and played with my emotions like the skilled playboy he was.

My skeleton man. That was what I had named him. The dark vigilante in a mask who helped save my life. Twice.

If this was any other place besides this strip club, I would have enjoyed my crush coming to my aid. But tonight? No. He was going to ruin *everything*.

The bouncers never moved in our direction. Maybe they thought I had it under control. Or perhaps they were bored. I wasn't sure, but it cemented my suspicion that they weren't there for the girls. The management hired them for muscle, just not for the front room.

31

"Hey, back off. Both of you." I lifted my empty tray, holding it between me and Skel. "No fighting. And there's no touching unless I say so," I added, glaring at both men.

The guy on the floor apologized, nursing his bruising jaw as he sat there. Maybe he was too smashed to get up.

Skel cocked a brow, daring me to ignore him.

I did it anyway, rushing toward the bar. After placing the tray down, I made a beeline for the ladies' room.

Skel caught me first. His arms slid around me and lifted, carrying me into the empty storage room instead. I wiggled out of his embrace before he shut the door behind us, leaning against the wood with a scowl.

No mask tonight. I almost missed it.

"What the fuck are you doing here, Lacey?"

"I don't owe you any explanations."

"Tell me. Now," he ordered in a gruff voice, pushing off the door to step closer.

"Why do you care? Huh?"

"Caring about you was never the issue."

Oh, really? "Enlighten me, then, Mr. Big Bad Biker. What's the issue between us?"

Yeah, I was taunting him. I wanted Skel to feel just half of the agony I felt when he broke up with me. Or, to be more precise, when he stopped us from having a relationship before it could become something deep or permanent.

"Lacey."

"I'm listening."

He shook his head. "Age difference. Lifestyle. That's the first two."

"Bullshit." Those were excuses, not valid reasons.

"You callin' me a liar, baby?"

Skel looked pissed, but the heat in his gaze wasn't from the insult alone. That fire that burned between us whenever we were close, the attraction that blazed as hot as a five-alarm fire, always flared at the wrong time.

"No. I'm calling you a *coward*," I taunted.

His dark eyebrows shot up briefly. I surprised him. People probably didn't try to piss off a tatted, muscled, six-foot-four behemoth of a man wearing a motorcycle vest often. Bet he never had anyone talk to him the way I did. Good.

He needed to be brought down a peg or two from that high steel horse he sat on. *Handsome, arrogant fucker.*

"A coward," he repeated, his voice low and menacing.

Shit. "Yes. If you weren't so afraid to commit—"

"Gonna stop you right there, my spoiled little goddess. Commitment ain't an issue either."

I couldn't figure him out. No matter what I said or did, he just kept coming back for more. Only, it wasn't consistent. He popped in and out of my life like a damn yo-yo whenever it suited his whim. Then he just disappeared three years ago after that whirlwind romance we had, only to show up again now. I hated that I fell for him and couldn't stop my heart from loving a man who didn't want to stick around.

"This is pointless," I sighed. "Move out of my way."

His lips twitched, and I couldn't tell if it was a grin or a threat as he cracked his knuckles.

"Baby, you're gonna regret all of this."

My gaze swept over Skel's numerous facial tattoos, including a spider and a blade pointing down his left cheek. A giant skeleton was inked across his right arm from shoulder to wrist. Skulls, flames, and other designs dominated his upper body.

He had so much dark ink it took up almost all the available space, stretching from beneath his chin to both wrists and down his torso to above his pubic bone.

I heard it was painful to tattoo over thin skin and figured he must have a high pain tolerance.

How did I know how far that tattoo dipped above his groin?

Because this gorgeous outlaw fucked me more than once, and I loved every minute. *Stop thinking about it, Lacey.*

Skel reached into his vest pocket and pulled out his mask. He winked before tugging it on, staring at me through the eyes that made him feel more like a predator than a man.

I should have run when I had the chance. By the time I remembered what he said, I bolted for the door, too late to reach it. Skel was fast. Strong arms surrounded me and lifted high, carrying me to a heavy wooden barrel where Skel sat. His hands settled on my hips and dared me to fight him.

"Don't try that again, Lacey."

His fingers lightly caressed my skin as they drifted to my navel. For a few seconds, neither of us moved. Skel reached for the button on my jean shorts and popped them open, ripping the zipper down as I smacked at his hands. It had zero effect on him.

He left my panties on. The shorts were yanked off.

My body tipped as he pushed me over his lap, and my stomach rested on his hard, thick thighs. I squirmed and fought him, realizing he was about to do something humiliating and painful. Oh. My. God. *He wouldn't.*

"Don't you dare!" I shouted. "Someone could come in here any minute!"

"Anyone comes in this door, and I'll fucking kill them," he growled.

I believed him.

The harder I fought, the more he seemed to enjoy it. It wasn't hard to miss the bulge growing in his jeans since my abdomen butted against his groin.

"Please," I begged, wincing before he began.

"Sweet Girl, we gotta work this out. You don't insult me. You don't sass me unless you want this to happen."

"Okay," I relented. "I'm sorry."

"Apology accepted."

I didn't expect to feel the sting of his slap only two seconds after his reply. "Hey!" I screeched. "That hurt!"

"It's not over yet, Darlin'."

Two more followed, harder than the first. My butt felt like it was on fire. Heat bloomed on my cheeks as I whimpered. "Please."

"You're such a good girl, Lacey. Look at you, squirming on my lap like this."

Another slap followed as he groaned.

"Skel. Please!"

He began to massage my sore bottom, and I rolled my hips, liking his touch far too much even if it hurt to be spanked.

Shit. It wasn't just the slaps getting to me. It was the idea of him bending me over to spank me and that we could get caught. That nothing prevented someone from walking in and that Skel would kill to protect me. He already did it three years ago. Why was that so fucking hot?

His palm rubbed the naked, exposed flesh, soothing the inflamed skin on my ass. "Damn. Baby, you're all wet."

I groaned as I wiggled on his lap, hating that he was right.

"Is it the pain or my touch that's turning you on? Hmm?"

I didn't answer.

A swift smack followed. "Answer me."

I couldn't help grinding against him, eager for his hand to move lower and dip between my thighs. Would he use his fingers or his mouth to make me come if I asked? "Both?" I answered, a little breathless. I could feel my body warming, growing needy as I gripped his pant legs.

"Since you're not sure, let's find out." He yanked on my underwear and ripped them away from my core, sliding two fingers through my slit and into my dripping pussy.

I jolted. A moan escaped as he began to pump in and out of me, still kneading one of my bottom cheeks with his other hand. The sounds my pussy made as he speared me proved it was the man in the mask who turned me on most.

"Fuck. You know what I'm thinking about right now?"

I couldn't reply, too lost to the sensations pulsing through my core and buzzing around my clit. Just a little more friction. It wouldn't take much to make me come.

We moved in tandem. Me, grinding and rocking against him, eager to find completion. Skel, thrusting his fingers in the same tempo, bringing me so fucking close.

"Skel," I whimpered with need.

"It's not my fingers you're gonna come on, Sweet Girl. I want your release on my tongue."

He pulled out his fingers as I protested, turning me so that I faced the barrel. My ass jutted out, and I heard his groan. "Fuck it. I need to feel you, Lacey. I can't hold back."

I heard him hesitate as he reached for his belt buckle, waiting for me to consent. A naughty part of me wanted to deny him, but that would only delay my own pleasure. I was too far gone for that little game. "Please. Fuck me, Skel."

"I love hearing that sweet little mouth talk like that."

The snap on his jeans popped, followed by the zipper being yanked down. I felt his body heat return to me, flush against my ass.

"Do you know how perfect and tight your pussy is? How much I want to fuck you until you're dripping with my cum, and it's glistening on your thighs?"

He notched the tip of his cock at my entrance. The first inch slid in, teasing me as he refused to thrust deep.

"Skel."

"I wish you could see how greedy your cunt is and how you suck me in, ready to swallow all of my cock. It's fucking addicting, my beautiful little tease."

I tried to move my hips, but he held me in place.

"Stay still. Enjoy the pounding I'm about to give you. Take every fucking hard inch, and don't say a word until you scream with your orgasm. You hear me, Baby?"

I did.

He gave my ass one last slap and drove so deep I rose on my tiptoes to accommodate his entire length. He took me hard and fast, thrusting so wildly that the wooden barrel rocked underneath my hands, and it had to weigh a ton with all the liquid inside.

It was impossible to remain completely silent. The way he owned my body and used me, giving and taking as he brought the both of us to the edge of delirium, nearly broke me.

My head wanted to forget he hurt me. My heart couldn't seem to stop thumping with the brutality of our past.

It was a stalemate. I'd loved Skel for three long years and didn't think I'd ever stop. But he didn't love me back. That was so painful that tears rushed to my eyes. A few slipped free, slinking over my cheeks as I got lost in my head, enjoying and hating this moment with Skel.

He must have sensed the change. Pulling out, he tugged me against his chest, his cock slipping between my thighs to tease my aching pussy from behind. "You left me."

"I didn't mean to," I whispered, unable to hide the sob that followed.

"Fuck." He turned me around as his eyes found mine through the holes in the mask. "I would never hurt you."

"Physically? No." I sniffled. "But you're breaking my heart every time you walk away."

The mask hid his expression. I didn't know what he thought or if I just pushed him away for good.

"I want to finish this and not leave you aching, Baby. This conversation isn't over. Will you trust me?"

I blinked as two more tears tracked down my cheeks. Skel wiped them away. "Yes."

"Wrap your legs around my waist," he softly ordered as he lifted me. "You feel so fucking good, Lacey. Focus on how we fit together because we're fucking perfect."

Did he know what he said? What he admitted?

I love you, Skel.

My skeleton man. My dark knight on his iron horse. Skel was everything I ever wanted, every wicked fantasy and every schoolgirl dream. Without him, I was incomplete.

He entered me on an upward thrust, snatching my thoughts away as my body responded to his. It didn't take much for me to forget where we were or what was happening around us.

When Skel was near, I only wanted him.

He yanked the mask upward and lowered his head, capturing my lips in a kiss that stole my heart all over again. His dark hazel eyes filled with lust, but that wasn't the only thing I saw. Need and possessiveness warred for equal dominance.

"Come with me," he demanded, softening his tone. "Squeeze my cock and flood me, Baby. I want to see you fall apart."

It only took three more thrusts before I cried out his name, digging my nails into his shoulders as my core clenched, and I came so hard that I almost pushed him out.

Skel shuddered, slamming into me before he groaned. I felt his cock jerk inside me, and I held him close, not wanting the moment to end. We didn't move for a full minute, both of us panting as our breathing slowed.

He kissed me, brushing the hair out of my eyes. "Come on. We need to talk."

"Okay," I swallowed, brushing my fingertips over his jaw.

He helped me into my shorts, and I didn't miss the feral look in his eyes when he noticed the slick skin of my thighs smeared with our combined fluids.

ROYAL BASTARDS MC

Chapter 5

SKEL

THREE YEARS EARLIER

IT HAD BEEN FOUR days since I brought Lacey home and left her at the penthouse with her father. I spent that time digging deep into the web, searching for information on Juan and Luis Diego. The brothers shared a rap sheet a mile long. They'd been in trouble since their teen years, and both had seen the inside of a jail cell numerous times.

That concerned me. Judge Maxwell was targeted because of his reputation for being tough on crime. He was a notorious judge known for giving the maximum sentences to criminals. He already sent two of Luis Diego's associates to prison in the last year, including a cousin. That made Judge Maxwell an enemy of Luis and Juan Diego. By association, that also made Lacey a target. Luis took her to prove a point. He could get to her whenever he wanted, and if the judge sent his brother away, he would go after Lacey—an eye for an eye.

Men like Luis only knew violence. It was their way of life, the currency they used to evoke fear, and how they remained in control. Power was everything to Luis.

I had to strip him of it. That was the only way Lacey would be safe. I had to ensure his business dealings fell through, his men doubted his leadership, and his associates got spooked.

With a few strokes of the keys on my desktop computer, I set things in motion, knowing I had just created a shit storm and placed myself on a hit list. It wasn't wise to get involved in this bullshit, but I couldn't walk away, not after meeting Lacey and finding her in that cemetery.

Luis Diego could have harmed her much worse than he did. He frightened and intimidated her, but he didn't rape or beat her. I knew his type. That would happen next if I didn't stop him. Men like him didn't back down until they got what they wanted.

I'd fucking kill that motherfucker if he touched Lacey again, which meant I was involved now, and there was no turning back. My years in the Marine Corps prepared me for dealing with my enemies. I faced men far more ruthless when I was stationed overseas. Luis Diego didn't scare me. He was a boy trying to fight like a man.

He would regret his choices.

I pushed away from my desk and stood, stretching as I headed into the kitchen to rinse an empty coffee mug. Now that I had set things in motion on my end, I needed to talk to Lacey. She would want to know how my research was progressing, and I felt she needed to understand that this mess with Luis would escalate before it was over.

I offered my services as a P.I., but that wasn't all I intended. She needed my protection. Her father was powerful but couldn't protect her from Luis Diego or his men.

Luis would have to be put down like a rabid dog. If that opportunity happened on my watch, I wouldn't hesitate.

I didn't enjoy snuffing out a man's life, but sometimes there wasn't much choice. Some people were just evil.

I'd done vicious things in my life to protect innocents. Helping Lacey was just another mission. I wouldn't fucking fail.

I didn't have her number, so I decided to head back to her building, hoping I could get inside and take the elevator up to the penthouse. If I got lucky, she'd be home. I planned to ask her to dinner and to go over all of the information I had learned.

After a quick shower, I dressed in dark jeans and a black hoodie since the weather had grown cool and crisp. I stuffed my phone, wallet, and mask in my pockets, rushing out the door with a singular focus in mind. Lacey. She'd become almost an obsession since I met her.

A young woman far too vulnerable, in danger, and fucking gorgeous. All the traits that attracted a guy like me. I might not be a criminal, but I wasn't a saint either.

I lived my life the same way my old man did—a vigilante and outlaw, taking justice into my hands when necessary. The military bred me for war. My father prepared me for life. The combination? A ruthless, cunning, intelligent Marine who never backed down from a fight.

I retired from the Corps, but I never stopped training. The minute I ceased to use my skills, I'd become weak. That wasn't an option.

So, I wasn't sure what led me back to Lacey other than the need to keep her safe. I was too fucking old for her. Too set in my ways. I had nearly fifteen years on her, and it should make me sick to think of her like I did. I wasn't.

Lacey intrigued me. She turned me on. But it was her intelligence and resilience I found sexy. She didn't cower or hide or break down when Luis took her.

Some people shut down when confronted with extreme stress and violence. The shock proved to be too much. Lacey didn't. She stayed strong, persevered, and refused to panic.

She was fucking fierce. Goddamn, that made my cock hard.

When I rolled to a stop outside her building, I shut down my bike's engine and rose off the seat, eager to see Lacey. I didn't reach the entrance before she walked out, staring at her phone instead of paying attention to her surroundings.

We'd have to discuss that. She needed to learn situational awareness and how to identify potential threats or hazards. It was an important skill to master for making effective decisions and responding to danger. I could teach her all about it.

She didn't notice me yet, so I slipped my mask over my head. The advantage of being so close to Halloween was all the parties and costumes. People didn't alert to my mask around this time of year. It was easy to brush it off as a Halloween gimmick. It wasn't.

I adapted to civilian life after both my tours overseas and the twenty years I gave to my country. I learned to adjust my routine. But a part of me would always enjoy the anonymity of hiding my identity and observing from the shadows. It saved me the explanation or headache of dealing with the public.

Lacey finished texting whoever she messaged and slid her phone into her purse. Her head lifted, and she locked eyes with me. Or, more accurately, the mask. "Skel."

My name left her lips with a sweet gasp.

"Lacey. We need to talk."

She tilted her head to the side and bit her lip. "I've got to make an appearance at a Halloween party."

"Then I'll come with you."

She nodded. "Good. I could use someone with your skills."

My body stiffened, suddenly alert. "Have you received any threats?"

She smirked. "No. I just might need a reason to escape all the spoiled offspring of the powerful elite."

Ugh. "Why don't we skip and go for a ride instead?"

She seemed to consider it. "I wish I could, Skel. Or should I say Bran? But I promised my dad. It's not wise to piss him off when he's stressed. Besides, I don't want to add to his worry."

Good point. My gaze swept over her outfit, and I was glad she couldn't see my face. I didn't doubt that the lust trying to fog my brain would have been obvious. She looked delicious, tempting, and downright fuckable.

Lacey dressed in a French Maid costume. *Fuck me.*

Every young man's fantasy, including mine, with a curve-hugging dress, plunging neckline, a matching ribbon choker, and a headpiece. The skirt was too fucking short and the top too tight across her tits, pushing them together, or maybe that was just the type of bra she wore. I wanted to rip off the costume and find out. She wore fishnet stockings and black heels. Her blonde hair had been pinned back from her face and cascaded over her slender shoulders.

What a fucking knockout.

"You're wearing that?" I asked, trying to keep the grit and possessiveness from leaking through since I only wanted to shove her back inside and make her change. No one should be staring at her like she was a sweet treat to gobble up, including me. Fuck.

If any motherfucker tried to touch her tonight, I'd have to set them straight. With my fists, my boot up their ass, or whatever it took to send the message: *Mine.*

Well, shit. I didn't plan on growing so overprotective or needing Lacey as intensely as I did. This was fucked.

"What's wrong with my costume?" She spun in a circle, bouncing her tits in the process. They almost burst free from the top.

Fuckkkkkkk.

"Nothing," I growled. "Let's go. Ass on my bike. Now, Lacey."

She bit her lip, accurately guessing my issue. Not that I hid it well when my cock swelled and pressed into my zipper.

For fuck's sake, I was growing hard just from staring at her like I was fifteen again and noticed a pretty girl in school.

"You okay, Skel?" She squeezed my bicep before she made a show of bending over to straddle my bike. Her palms rested on the leather as her ass jutted out. With agonizing slowness, she hiked a leg over the seat and caught my gaze, holding it as she dragged her bottom backward, only stopping when she met the edge of the seat.

My hands clenched. I was almost panting, nearly salivating with the idea of fucking her right here, in front of the whole fucking City of Sin, and I didn't give a fuck.

Any good intentions I had vanished after that. Before the night was over, I'd be buried deep in her pussy. She'd know what it was like to be with a man, and I was damn sure I'd ruin her for any other guy.

She would know the truth before I brought her home. Lacey was gonna be mine. Why fight the inevitable?

The ride to the Halloween party was the longest in fucking existence. A torment I would gladly repeat if my dick wasn't throbbing with the idea of slipping a hand between her thighs and feeling the silky soft folds of her pussy. I bet she tasted sweet and tangy, forbidden and exotic.

"Skel? You keep growling," Lacey pointed out as we idled at a red light.

"I'm good."

She giggled. I wasn't fucking good. I was about to explode.

By the time we arrived and parked, I was jacked up, horny as fuck, and far too tense to do more than let her lead me inside. I glanced at all the expensive cars in the lot and the affluent neighborhood. I didn't fit in here, but I liked that.

Lacey and I came from two different worlds. It should have made me pause, but I only grew more obsessed.

46

The banquet hall had been decorated for the spooky season, and the dim lights helped calm me as they somewhat disguised Lacey's assets. A fog machine pumped creepy waves of smoke into the massive room. Carved pumpkins were placed throughout, along with bats, spiders, and other various Halloween decorations.

Whoever set this up didn't hold back. Music from various horror movies trickled through speakers while flashing lights and purple bulbs added to the mysterious, haunting vibe.

One section had been draped with spiderwebs and black cloth. Several tables loaded with treats like pretzels, chips, sandwiches, and popcorn provided snacks for anyone hungry beyond the need for sugar.

A woman dressed like the bride of Frankenstein served punch from an enormous claw-footed bowl. The vampire beside her ladled lemonade from a cauldron into plastic cups. I spotted the bar and steered Lacey toward the adult beverages.

"Thirsty?" I asked, ticking my chin toward one of the bartenders. Several worked the crowd and wore costumes: a werewolf, a Jedi, and a grim reaper.

Two guys were running around wearing inflatable dicks. I slid my arm around Lacey's waist and hugged her against me.

She giggled. "Funny. Did you see one of them had white stuff on the tip?"

I did. "Yeah, Sweet Girl. What do you want to drink?"

"A Long Island iced tea."

I ordered hers first and then two shots of whiskey and a beer. When I spotted the attention that she was receiving from other men, I knew I needed liquor to calm down and attempt to relax. Not that it would happen. I probably wouldn't feel less keyed up until my cock was buried inside her.

I tossed back both shots after handing over her tea. Lifting my bottle, I steered her toward a table in the corner. If I could keep my hands on her, maybe I'd feel less volatile.

We sat, and I pulled her onto my lap, ignoring her gasp of surprise. She squirmed, and I stilled her hips, both hating and loving how her warm center pressed into my groin.

"Lacey. Stop, Baby."

She gave me a coy smile. "We both know that's not what you want."

Fuck. Little vixen. "You're playing a dangerous game, my bold little hellion."

"What if it's not a game?" She turned and wrapped her arms around my neck. "What if I want you as much as you want me? I can feel your erection, Skel. That bulge is promising to give me what I'm missing. Are you going to deny it?"

Fuck. Me.

"You know I can't."

"Then kiss me."

"Here? You don't want to go somewhere more private?"

I knew once I had her lips, I would want all of her. She would feel too damn good to stop.

My gaze swept over the table and the wall beside us. Tucked into the corner, we had plenty of privacy or we would in a moment. The strands of lights above our heads cast enough glow to light up our movements, but if I unplugged them . . .

I didn't hesitate to reach over and yank them out. We were plunged into darkness, the corner concealing anything we might do with so many others in the room. I shoved my mask upward, leaving it on my head.

Lacey's lips met mine as I tugged her closer, turning to face me as she straddled my lap. "It's just you and me, Skel. Don't hold back."

"Last chance, Lacey."

"To do what?" she asked in a husky tone. "Tell me."

"That's what you like, huh, Dirty Girl?"

My pretty blonde temptress liked to walk on the wild side. It turned her on to know that we could get caught. I had to admit it fucking made me grow harder just thinking of ripping into those tights and shoving her panties aside, thrusting my cock into her tight pussy while the party raged around us.

Her hips began to sway against me, and I gripped her waist, sliding my palms backward to cup her ass beneath the skirt. So fucking soft. So goddamn greedy for me.

I couldn't keep my hands or my mouth off her. She tasted like sweet temptation and hungry sin, like freshly picked apples and bourbon-laced caramel.

I couldn't help comparing her to those store-bought candy apples that appeared every fall dipped in a sweet, thick sauce and rolled in peanuts—my favorite autumn dessert as a kid.

But she was even sweeter and more delicious.

"Sweet Girl, I'm going to fuck you. Right here at this party. You don't want that, it's your only chance to stop me."

Her breath hitched as her eyes widened. She panted as I rolled my body upward, driving my jean-clad cock into her core.

Say yes, my sexy little maid. I need to make you come.

Just say yes.

ROYAL BASTARDS MC

Chapter 6

LACEY

PRESENT

SKEL'S HAND HELD MINE in an iron grip, not allowing anyone to deter us as we left the storage room and headed straight for the exit of the strip club. My head still buzzed with post-orgasm bliss, and I wished I could have spent five more minutes in his arms before he made his excuses and left me behind. Again.

I could feel his cum drying on my thighs and sticking to my denim shorts as we walked, reaching the exit as one of the bouncers blocked our way. A big Russian guy who spoke broken English and rarely moved from his post.

"No."

I felt Skel stiffen, ready to argue. "She wants to leave."

"Not on the clock."

Shit. I didn't think of that. "I'm not feeling well. I already cleared it with Rosemary."

Rose worked in the back, mainly as a secretary. She was hard as nails and twice as sharp. No one did shit without running it by her first. Even the Russian understood the management protected her. If she said I could leave, he wouldn't stop me.

Of course, I never actually spoke to Rose. That was a lie.

The Russian grunted. "Go."

He stepped aside as Skel nearly dragged me out the front, ordering me onto his bike as he watched the door for trouble, firing up the engine while he sat. "Hold on tight, Lacey."

I snuggled closer, wrapping my arms around his waist as the Harley's deep base rumble awakened like a slumbering beast beneath us. My entire body vibrated with its cadence, and I knew I'd never felt anything sexier or more alive than this bike and its rider.

"We're headin' to my place."

Skel's house? I hadn't gone back there since the night I was attacked. For the *second* time. He saved my life twice, and maybe I couldn't see beyond the gratitude I felt or the safety he evoked whenever he was around. But that wasn't quite true. When I was near Skel, everything inside me sparked to life. He made me feel beautiful, sexy, desired and wanted. Things every woman needed.

The ride to his place took fifteen minutes. When we arrived, Skel pushed the button for his garage door, gliding up the driveway to park inside. He didn't waste time closing it, staring out into the night like he wondered if we'd been followed.

"Everything okay?"

He shook his head. "No."

I didn't know what to say to that, so I let him lead, allowing Skel to curl his fingers around mine and pull me into his house. The décor hadn't changed much in three years. All the furniture was the same, but I spotted a new abstract painting in the room he used for an office since he'd left the door open.

Once inside, he released my hand to walk into the kitchen, leaving me alone in the living room. Without his warmth, I began to shiver. The wind had been cold, and I didn't have a jacket. I wore only a tight tank top and jean shorts. I'd managed to remember my purse but nothing else.

A blanket draped my shoulders as Skel returned and wrapped the soft material around me. "You're cold."

"Yes. Thank you."

No detail ever escaped his notice when I was around. It was intoxicating how he seemed attuned to me. God, he owned me without any effort at all.

"Come on." He steered me toward one of his dark gray couches since the two faced one another, separated by only a black coffee table. "Sit. Get warm."

I obeyed, taking a spot on the end of the closest one and burrowing into the blanket.

"I'm going to build a fire."

I didn't protest. The room was chilly. Skel threw a few logs in his fireplace and lit a starter, crouching to coax the embers into flames. Heat began to fill the room as he stood, brushing his hands on his thighs.

"Tell me why you're working at that strip club, Lacey. And no bullshit."

I couldn't help sighing at his brisk tone. "I'm working with the police."

Yeah, he didn't expect that answer. His shoulders rolled before he cracked his neck, striding toward me with a thunderous frown. "The fuck? Why?"

"Because Luis Deigo and Angel Mackenzie traffic girls through Las Vegas, and I'm trying to help stop them."

Skel dropped beside me on the couch. His jaw clenched before he answered me. I could see the tick in the muscle. "Baby, you're done with this. No fucking way are you going back there and ending up a fucking statistic."

I flinched. One, because he didn't have a right to order me to do a damn thing. Two, because he'd have to care about me to react this way. And three, he never sold his house or moved out, and I just realized what that meant.

"Let me clarify," I began, narrowing my eyes as I dropped the blanket and held up my hand, ticking off each of the things I figured out. "You're ordering me to stop the case I'm working on even though you left without offering help when I needed you the most. You act like I didn't mean anything to you after we fucked, but your controlling behavior is a contradiction."

He scoffed.

I gestured to the room, glaring at Skel. "And you haven't moved or sold your place but said you were leaving Vegas for good. Now you show back up, invade my life, and pretend you don't have any motive for doing it. So who is acting shady as fuck, huh?"

The timing for this argument was awful. Skel's cum had dried on my skin. I could feel it on my inner thighs as I sat on his cushion, feeling stupid and far too exposed. It always happened this way with him, giving in to my body's desires and needs instead of being rational.

"Lacey."

I refused to look at him.

"Baby, give me those pretty eyes."

I lifted my gaze, noting how he no longer appeared angry.

"I fucked up. It's not an excuse. I know I hurt you, and I never wanted that."

Swallowing hard, I nodded.

"For that, I'm sorry. It's the reason I walked away. I thought you were better off without my interference." He reached for my hand and held it. "Your father made it clear that he didn't want a murderer around his daughter. I've got blood on my hands. It's not fair to you."

"My dad told you to leave, didn't he?" I spat, shaking off his hand and rising to my feet in frustration. "You should have spoken to me, Skel. Walking away without hearing what I felt or wanted first wasn't okay."

"You were so young, Lacey. Still in college."

That wasn't a denial that my father had words with him.

"So? I still know my mind and heart, Bran. I'm not a child."

To get the point across, I used his real name instead of the alias he'd been given as a Marine. The same road name he adopted when he became a biker. I saw the patches on his leather vest and knew what they meant. He was a member of a motorcycle club.

"No, you're not." Skel lifted his hands, resting his palms against my cheeks. "Sweet Girl, you're my pleasure and my pain. There's not a day I don't wake up thinking of you."

"Is that why you came back to Las Vegas?"

No. I could see it in his eyes—the pain of the truth. I had nothing to do with the reason he returned.

Shit. "I see."

"I came back for Maddog, my new president. The club needed me." He stared into my eyes, clearly tortured. "I didn't want to hope that you would still care for me, Lacey. Time forced a wedge between us, and that's my fault."

But he was wrong about my feelings. My heart ached for him as intently now as it did three years ago. I still wanted to be with him. Didn't he feel it when we had sex in the storage room?

"You were crying back there," he continued, guessing where my thoughts had taken me, "Tell me why."

"Because it doesn't matter how much I care about you, Skel. You still won't stay with me."

He closed his eyes, breathing a heavy sigh. They slowly opened as he shook his head. "I fucked this all up."

I stepped back, and his hands fell away. "There's not much point in continuing this conversation. I need to go home."

"Lacey," he began to argue as the power shut off, and we plunged into darkness. Only the fireplace provided enough light to keep us from a total blackout.

"Skel?"

He glanced out the windows. "Fuck."

"What's happening?"

"It's only us." Skel grabbed my hand and led me to the hallway, rushing into his office. "I've got a panic room behind the bookshelves. Stay in there, lock it from the inside, and don't open the door for anyone other than me. Promise me, Lacey."

"Okay," I whispered, blinking as he pulled out a book and flipped a switch in the vacant spot.

The bookcase separated from the wall, and he shoved it open, gesturing for me to duck down. "You have to climb in. There are monitors to see what's happening. Stay quiet. If someone finds you, use one of the guns. Don't hesitate."

"I'm scared," I admitted as I heard a window break. The glass shattered, and I knew we weren't alone.

Skel smashed his mouth to mine, giving me a kiss before pushing me into the panic room. "You're safe," he whispered as he closed the door behind me, and I heard it locking into place. I saw additional security latches and used them, hoping that meant that I prevented someone from opening the secret door.

The room was small. Four walls, a carpeted floor, and a few crates of supplies. There was a desk with several monitors that blipped between images, all showing different angles of Skel's house. Spinning in a circle, I noticed the room had been well stocked. Keeping quiet, I searched through everything. A mini fridge provided cold drinks. One of the crates held dry goods and snacks like trail mix, protein bars, and peanut butter.

The furniture consisted of the desk with monitors, an office chair, a small couch, the crates, and a table with two folding chairs. Searching through the remaining crates, I found blankets, pillows, and extra clothing. Underneath the desk, I spotted a safe and a thick wooden case. I opened it, finding a handgun and ammo. Wow. This just got real.

The dark room was cool, and I took one of the blankets, wrapping myself up before I sat in the office chair, staring at the monitors. I shouldn't have looked. My fingers trembled when I saw proof we weren't alone in Skel's house.

Three men wearing black clothes and ski masks had entered the house. One stood inside Skel's office, just feet from where I hid behind the bookcase. He scanned the whole area, taking far too long to leave.

Terrified, I slowly rose to my feet and pushed the chair away from me. I sat on the floor, keeping the monitor in view as I reached for the gun case. If he found a way to open the bookcase, I would use the gun.

The criminal wore an oversized hoodie pulled low to disguise his features. He circled the room, searching for something as he tossed chairs around and sent the contents of Skel's desk to the floor. I heard something break.

Where was Skel? I looked through each of the monitors but didn't see him. Was he hurt?

Just when I thought it couldn't get worse, another guy joined the first one in the office. Twice the threat. They turned toward the bookcase, and I froze, wondering if they knew Skel had a panic room.

Oh, shit. Shit. Shit!

Guns aimed in my direction, and I lowered to the ground, trying to lay as flat as possible. The bookcase and thin layer of drywall weren't enough barriers to stop bullets. Maybe slow them down if I was lucky but that was it. There was nothing to hide behind, but I could move toward the couch. Sliding in that direction, I remained low, taking refuge as far to the right as I could. From this angle, I couldn't see the monitor.

I sucked in a breath, trying not to panic. If I began wheezing, I didn't have my inhaler. I just needed to remain calm.

I'm safe. They can't reach me. Skel is out there, and he'll protect me.

I repeated the mantra in my head, determined not to break down or alert the men on the other side of the wall. I could do this. Skel would return to the office before they could find or hurt me.

My confidence shattered when the two men opened fire.

ROYAL BASTARDS MC

Chapter 7

SKEL

THREE YEARS EARLIER

Lacey tilted her hips, grinding on my cock as I groaned. All that separated us was a bit of fabric. Her short French Maid dress and fishnet stockings. My jeans. Nothing but sin and need runnin' through us both. Her warm breath fell across my skin as she moaned in my ear, caressing the back of my neck with the pads of her fingers.

I never wanted a woman as badly as I did at this moment. "Fuck, Baby. You make the sexiest noises when you're turned on."

She wasn't paying attention to my words. Desire ruled her every thought. Distracted, she whined.

"God, Skel. I need you. Fuck me. Please."

Jesus Christ. This girl. She never stopped surprising me.

If she wanted me to fuck her at this party, I was doing it.

"Take me out," I ordered low, watching as she licked her lips.

Her hands slid between us as she reached for the buckle on my belt, loosening the leather before she slid the strap free. A quick pop of the button on my jeans and then the zipper lowered. Her hand reached into my underwear and gripped me. One stroke slid from root to tip, and I bucked my hips in response. She did it again.

My head fell back. Fuck. Her soft touch grew bolder as she began to pump me harder, my rigid dick swelling even more. My hips snapped with her movements as my cock grew eager. She double-fisted me and I nearly saw stars. *Aw, fuck.* She'd make me cum like this.

I needed inside her before I shot my load.

"Skel. You're so thick."

"Not changin' your mind, are you?" *Please say no.*

"No way. I want you, Skel."

"The feeling is mutual," I murmured, removing her hands from my dick and placing them on my shoulders. She'd need them for leverage when I began fucking her. Party or not, I wasn't going to be gentle once I had her slick and ready.

She rocked her hips as I cupped her pussy, grabbing the crotch of her fishnet tights and ripping a hole through the material. I shoved the satin of her panties aside, sliding through her slick folds.

"This pussy is sopping wet for me, huh, Baby?"

She glanced away shyly.

"Hey, none of that. You fucking own this. Tell me what you want."

"You," she answered boldly.

"In detail," I growled.

"I want your cock inside me." If the lights had been on, I would have bet she blushed.

"And after I'm inside you?"

"Make me cum."

"In front of all these people?"

"Yeah."

"You're scandalous, Sweet Girl. Naughty little thing. I think you need a new nickname."

"Like what?" She panted but tried not to move, knowing I was seconds from thrusting into her.

I grasped my erection, lining up the crown with the entrance to her pussy. "My seductress," I groaned, driving upward to spread her cunt open, filling her with every hard inch of my cock.

Lacey moaned, and I took her mouth, trying to hide the fact that I was fucking her in a corner at a Halloween party. Best choice I ever fucking made. Her pussy closed around me, stretching to accommodate the girth and length of my dick. She was so fucking tight. I had to fight for control over my body and the urge to take her hard and fast.

"You're so big, Skel," she whispered as her nails dug into my shoulders. I felt her tense.

"You can take me," I assured her. "I'll go slow."

"Okay," she whimpered, letting me set the pace.

With every thrust, I went deeper until I filled her. I built my strokes, each one burying my dick before I retreated, only to thrust back in, the motion growing slicker and easier as she began to relax.

"That's it. Good girl," I praised, capturing her lips again.

The kiss was wild and needy. We lashed tongues. Bumped teeth. And I nipped at the swollen flesh before I held her jaw in place as I pumped harder, slamming into her pussy with every downward plunge of her hips. My free hand guided her movements, holding onto her ass as I pulled her onto me.

"This feels so good, Skel."

Yeah, it did. Best sex I'd had in a long time. Probably the best I ever had. Lacey was so responsive. Her little moans and breathy sighs. The way she took me, eager, swaying her hips as she chased her orgasm. Her wet and tight pussy.

"I'm going to come."

Goddamn. I wanted to feel her lose control. The dark corner prevented me from watching her fall apart as I fucked her, but next time, I wanted to see it.

"Then come. Let me feel you clench my cock."

A low moan escaped before she stilled, crying my name as I stole it from her lips. I felt her spasm around me and milk my dick, squeezing as her orgasm released.

Halloween music still pumped through the speakers, but I could hear the slap of flesh on flesh and her soft cries. If anyone moved close enough to us, they'd know what we were doing. It excited me even more.

"Lacey," I groaned, shuddering as I spilled into her, coating her walls with my cum and loving every second of it. She felt fucking amazing, perfect, and I didn't want to pull out or end this moment.

She clung to me in the darkness, panting as her head lowered to my neck. Her warm breaths blanketed my skin.

I held her to me, finally easing my dick out of her and realizing I was still semi-erect. My cock wanted another round with her.

"I can feel you dripping out of me," she admitted as she kissed the side of my face. "Is it bad that I love it?"

Fuckkkkk. No. It was sexy as fuck. "Not at all."

"I probably leaked all over your jeans."

Just one sentence, and I needed inside her again. "That's a problem, Sweet Girl."

"Why?"

"Because now I want to fuck you again."

She sucked in a breath. "Do it."

I plunged back into her, grabbing onto her waist to lift her up and down on my cock. It wasn't soft or sweet this time. I drove up into her a few more times before lifting her off me.

A tiny whine left her lips.

"I'm not done, Beautiful." I turned her around, bending her over as her palms rested on the table. "Try to be quiet," I ordered through a slight lull in the music, thrusting into her before she could reply.

I'd forgotten about our drinks and heard something fall, crashing to the floor right as the music started up again. I didn't care; I was too driven by my need for Lacey.

She rocked back against my thighs, taking every brutal plunge of my cock as I felt her tremble. Fuck. I wanted to see her ass as I slammed into her from behind.

It wasn't long, only a few deep snaps of my hips, before she came a second time. When I felt her clench around me, I lost control. My cock twitched inside her, and I shuddered as I filled her, knowing one night with Lacey would never be enough. I'd only gotten a taste.

I needed more. A hell of a lot more.

She didn't move as I withdrew, tucking my cock back into my jeans and zipping up. I fixed my belt and reached for her, drawing her back onto my lap.

Lacey rested her head on my shoulder, and I smoothed her skirt around her hips to cover the ripped fishnet tights and her bottom. "I think you wore me out."

I held her to me, ignoring the party as I heard people talking a short distance away.

"I think that couple in the corner is fucking."

My lips twitched. *Yeah, twice. I'm a lucky bastard.*

"Did you see who it was?"

"No."

"I saw a French Maid costume."

"There's a dozen of those here tonight."

They moved on, too far for me to overhear the rest.

"Skel?"

"Yeah, Sweet Girl?"

"Is your real name Bran?"

Her question surprised me only because I had expected her to ask long before now. "Yep. My parents always called me Bran, but I was born Michael Brandon Myers."

"Michael Myers?" She giggled. "Like the horror movies?"

"Yeah," I snickered. "My father's favorite villain. We used to watch the series every October and a marathon on Halloween. He'd play it loud as kids stopped to trick-or-treat at our front door."

"That sounds fun."

"It was. My pops said it was fate that he named me Michael. Couldn't pass it up with the last name Myers."

"Is he still alive?"

"He is."

"I'm glad."

I squeezed her, not needing to reply about how I felt, but I knew she understood. We both lost our mothers but formed close relationships with our fathers—a bond we shared.

"You wanna get out of here?"

I didn't see her move but felt her adjust on my lap, sitting up before she kissed me. "Yeah. Take me to your place."

WHEN WE WALKED OUTSIDE, I noticed the temperature had plummeted. It was cold as fuck, and a light rain began to fall.

Lacey didn't have a jacket or anything to protect her from the weather. She'd freeze in that skimpy costume and thin fabric.

I usually kept an extra sweatshirt or change of clothes in my saddlebags. Life was unpredictable, and I liked to be prepared. As I reached inside to grab the sweatshirt, I noticed Lacey shivering. "Here. Wear this. It's not much, but it'll help."

"Thanks."

She lifted her arms, and I helped her pull it on, satisfied when I saw it was huge on her, covering her enough that I could get her home before she got soaked. Or so I thought. The clouds decided to open up as we stood there, and the rain fell in thick sheets, drenching us as she laughed.

"I guess we're too late."

"Nah. I'll build a fire as soon as we're back at my place."

I didn't see the guy rushing us until he was only a few feet from Lacey. A knife glistened in his hand as the streetlights bounced off the steel blade. My military training kicked in, and I didn't hesitate to act.

Without a care that he could slash me instead of Lacey, I dove into her attacker, knocking him onto the wet ground. Gravel and something sharp dug into my side as I landed, but I didn't care about the pain. All that mattered was keeping Lacey safe.

A fight ensued. The fucker tried to stab me with his knife, and I caught his wrist, applying pressure as he hollered. The knife clattered to the asphalt a short distance away as I began punching the attacker in the face, hoping to knock him out. He jabbed at my side, and I nearly howled with pain, wondering why it hurt so damn much.

Lacey was yelling but I didn't look at her. I couldn't. If I lost focus for even a second, he could gain the upper hand. That wasn't an option.

We rolled around as Lacey screamed, and a lightning bolt shot across the sky, followed by a loud crack of thunder. I worried about her out in the open, exposed to the elements, and far too vulnerable as I wrestled with the guy who'd come after her. What if he wasn't alone?

My fist connected with his jaw, and the back of his head slammed into the ground with a crack. He wouldn't be getting up anytime soon. I rolled him onto his side so the rain didn't drown him, grunting as the pain in my side intensified.

"Skel!"

I turned my head as I shot to my feet, worried that someone else had come after Lacey. My gaze swept over the parking lot. No one was there. Not even people attending the Halloween party. The rain had kept everyone indoors, forcing them to wait for the downpour to slow down before they headed to their cars.

I didn't see any other threats.

"Oh, God, Skel. You're bleeding!" She stared at me with wide, frightened eyes. "You're hurt."

I looked down, noticing the slash in my hoodie and the tee shirt underneath, watching as blood oozed from the wound.

That motherfucker stabbed me.

ROYAL BASTARDS MC

Chapter 8

SKEL

PRESENT

I LEFT LACEY IN the panic room as I reached for the guns in my office, taking several with me and extra ammo. I shoved one into the waistband of my jeans, palming the other as I heard someone moving through my living room. I had to steer whoever showed up away from my woman.

The house was so fucking dark. If I didn't know where everything was placed or where my guns were located, I would have stumbled into furniture or made too much noise. But I didn't. My head-mounted night vision goggles were stored inside the top drawer of my desk, and I snatched them, quickly slipping them on.

These ignorant fucks didn't comprehend who they were fucking with. I'd end every threat and spill blood without hesitation. My fucking property. My rules. *Fuck around and find out.*

The bright flashlight beam shined into the hallway, and I hid behind the door, staying still as it approached, swept the room, and moved on. How amateur. He didn't clear my office. His loss, my gain.

I checked the hall and entered, ensuring no one followed behind me. Following the flashlight as it searched my house, I crept behind the intruder. My mind focused on the task at hand instead of on Lacey. It wasn't easy, but I knew she was safe.

Outside, I heard thunder before a light rain began to plink against the windows. It reminded me of the night three years ago when I went to the Halloween party with Lacey and fucked her in a dark corner. Everything about that night had been perfect until we were attacked outside the banquet hall.

I'd been stupid to leave her for the last three years. Luis Diego had waited for the right moment to return, and now he was after Lacey again. This time, he wasn't holding back. Luis wanted my woman dead.

That would be his last mistake. Once I removed the intruders, I would handle this shit. I had to take it to the club. Maddog didn't know the whole story. Before I went vigilante, I had to fill my new pres in on the details.

This wasn't about the RBMC. It was personal.

I never truly left Vegas. I'd kept my house and visited friends. Even crashed a few times at Maddog's place. Breaking all ties with this town meant losing my connection to my brothers, whom I served with in the Corps, my father's legacy, and the brotherhood, which still meant everything to him, not to mention the woman I loved. I'd never let that happen.

I might have stopped seeing Lacey, but I never went far. The last night we were together, I installed an app that allowed me to track her phone location. I'd kept tabs on her, watching her routine, and made sure she was safe.

Until I came back.

In the last couple of weeks, I rarely checked the app, and now that was a fucking problem because I didn't know about her helping the police or working at a strip club. And now my home had been invaded.

We'd been followed. Or maybe Luis Diego already knew where I lived and waited for me to bring Lacey here. It didn't matter.

Breaking into my house was a death sentence.

The guy with the flashlight never heard me approach. I stored my gun in my belt and crept forward, wrapping my arm around his neck, and pushed on his carotid artery hard, knocking him out fast. He hit the ground, and I followed. Hoping the small thud didn't bring the others running.

I made quick work of subduing him, hoping I could question him at the clubhouse. Manic and Creature would enjoy that. Deciding I couldn't leave him out in the open for the others to find, I dragged him into a closet and shut the door. He was already regaining consciousness, but he wouldn't be able to do more than struggle against the zip ties and the thick tape I placed over his mouth. I'd come back for him.

Moving through my silent house, I carefully hunted the other two intruders. They weren't on the second floor, which meant I had to sneak downstairs. Gunfire alerted me to their location as I ran toward my office.

Lacey!

Two men opened fire on the bookcase, and I pulled out one of my guns, tapping the trigger twice in quick succession. Steady. Controlled. Perfectly aimed. Two matching bullets in two foreheads. *Lights out, motherfuckers!*

With no threats remaining, I opened the bookcase and swung it wide, hollering for Lacey. *Fuck, please don't let her be hurt.*

"Skel!" Her frightened cry had me ducking down and rushing inside the panic room, relieved to find her on the ground and uninjured. Her chest rose and fell as I heard her lungs wheeze.

Shit. She needed her inhaler.

"You were so fucking brave, Baby. Come here."

She launched into my arms as I held her against me, keeping my eye on the monitors in case of more trouble. "Where's your inhaler?"

"In my purse."

"Be right back." I left her long enough to grab what I needed and returned, pressing the medicine to her lips. She took two puffs and collapsed against me.

"Shhh," I soothed, wrapping my arms around her. "You're safe. I've got you, Lacey."

It took twenty minutes to calm her down enough for me to make a call. I dialed Maddog's number.

"Skel. What's up?"

"I need a cleaner."

"Shit. What the fuck happened?"

I explained the situation, pressing the end button after he promised to send Creature. I'd have help taking care of the bodies and cleaning up the mess. From men I trusted, which was crucial.

Lacey couldn't stay here. My place was compromised. She wasn't safe anywhere but the clubhouse or home with her dad. I knew she'd choose me, but she needed to fill her father in on everything happening.

I had to take her home. Temporarily.

The judge was in danger, and so was his daughter.

"Who were those men?" she asked, fighting back tears as I sank onto the couch, holding her in my lap.

"Diego's men. I'm sure of it."

"It's been years. Why come after me now?"

"I don't know, but you need to tell me everything, Lacey. I can't protect you if I don't know what the fuck is going down."

She sighed. "I know."

"Then speak up, Baby. Let me help you." I didn't tell her that I was taking her home yet.

Lacey trembled as I held her tighter.

Don't fall apart on me now, Sweet Girl.

"Um, I, uh," she stammered.

"Breathe, Baby. I'm right here."

She listened, calming enough to speak. "I didn't start out trying to help the police. It happened after I saw a story on the local news. Girls being trafficked, a burned truck with bodies, and a man wanted for connection to the murders."

"Luis Diego," I guessed.

"Yes. I swore vengeance on that asshole after he kidnapped me. I wanted him behind bars and went to the police precinct to speak to the detective in charge of the case. They said after he was released from prison, Luis went right back into his old life."

"Damn. Does your dad know about your involvement in this?"

She smirked. "Hell no. He would have lost his shit."

I bet.

"A case is being built against Luis, but they don't have enough to charge him yet. That's why I'm working at the strip club. The management thinks I'm playing at being a rebel to piss off my father, but I'm there to learn anything I can about Luis and his operation, including information about his partner, Angel Mackenzie."

Well, fuck. The club had a problem with Angel and Luis, too, primarily because of their connection to Ratchet, the president of the Bladed Serpents. But this put Lacey right in the middle of a war between clubs, a dangerous cartel, and a trafficking ring.

"You can't go back."

"Skel."

"No, you can't. It's too risky."

"But I'm the only one who can get close. Angel and Luis are supposed to arrive for a private party Friday night. There was a chance they'd show tonight. That's why I was working."

She didn't understand. I wasn't allowing this.

"Baby, you're not going back to that club. Don't you get it? Diego is back in town, and if he sees you at that club, he'll hurt you."

"But—"

"We'll find another way."

Her shoulders slumped. "How?"

"The club bought the strip club. We're going to remodel and clean it up, turn a profit, and keep the business legit."

She arched a brow. "Legit?"

"Fine. As legit as we can. It's fucking Vegas, Baby."

Her lips curled into a smile, but it quickly vanished. "I know."

"I'll meet with my pres. Fill him in on all this. But you're out of it. You need to stick close to home. Stay there and outta trouble." I sure hoped she would listen.

"This sucks, Skel. I've waited so long for revenge. This was my chance."

"We'll get him. I promise."

I never should have left the night I saved her life without telling Lacey what she meant to me. We ended up burning hot and fast, but that didn't mean what we shared was a fling. Far from it. I didn't stop thinking about her for three long years.

"Luis Diego won't stop until I'm dead, will he?"

"No. So that means we make the next move, keep you safe, and I handle Diego."

She swallowed hard. "My dad. He's in danger, too."

"That's why I'm taking you home. I'll talk to the judge as soon as I clean up here."

She buried her head in my neck. "Okay."

"IS IT DONE?" MADDOG asked as I parked my bike inside the lot of our new clubhouse.

It seemed fitting to use this property in Vegas. The old casino renovation had been a brilliant idea. We had plenty of space, and the original wood added a rich accent to the interior. Construction was coming along, and most of the rooms were in the drywall stage, which was ready for paint next week. The floors had been in great shape beneath all the old carpet, and Maddog opted to hire a company to refinish them. The building no longer resembled the late seventies hotel and casino, rundown, and vacant.

We just had a ton of electrical and remodeling to do with the bedrooms, bathrooms, and main floor. Maddog had shared the plans with us, which included a massive bar, industrial kitchen, and a chow hall that could feed over a hundred people in one sitting. It reminded me of our boot camp days without all the bullshit.

"It is," I answered, noting that he straddled his Harley.

"Good. We're takin' that ride, Skel. It's time."

"No church?"

"Not yet. You'll understand after we ride into the desert."

Yeah, I didn't get that part. That terrain could tear up my bike, and I hated getting a scratch on her. "Alright, pres."

I rode behind Maddog as he left the lot. Manic and Creature followed as a prospect closed the gate of our new fence behind us. It didn't take long to pass beyond the Strip and out of Vegas, heading down the highway until we turned onto a dirt road. After a few minutes, we veered off and turned right, crossing into the desert as our tires sped over hot sand.

Anyone who's ever traveled through the desert has learned about mirages. They spring up when least expected as a sheen of water across the sand. An optical illusion known to make men crazy with thirst when they've been in the sun too long.

So, I didn't trust the mirage I saw heading my way. It didn't seem like more than a dark blur until I rode closer, catching the image of a horse.

Not just *any* horse. A skeleton that moved with a grace that shouldn't be possible. No mane but fiery waves that resembled moving hair. He made a noise that sounded like tiny cracks of thunder and pawed at the air as his rider stopped him only a few feet from where I hit the brakes and skid, nearly colliding with the bony beast.

I stared at the being who dropped from the seat, dressed in a long flowing robe. Cinders crackled across the material as red eyes focused on me, glowing with a demonic hue. His hood hid his features as I peered inside. Was there a face hidden? Or only a monster in the shadows?

"Ah, at last, I meet the infamous Skeletor."

He knew my name. My road name, to be precise. The moniker I'd been given as a Marine because I always wore my skeletal mask overseas while on active duty. It kept the dust out of my nose and mouth and intimidated my enemies.

I narrowed my eyes, wondering if I'd fallen off my bike or crashed, and smacked my head. Was this a dream?

"Not a dream," the being chuckled. "You're here. I'm here. It's real."

Maybe. Still seemed a bit hazy like I was stuck in a nightmare and clawing to get out.

He snorted. "You amuse me."

"What do you want?" I glanced around us, no longer seeing Maddog, Manic, or Creature. "Where are my brothers?"

"Brothers in arms. Brothers in a club. You all enjoy your bromances, don't you?"

I shot him a look. "I don't fuck men." Not that I cared if anyone else did; it just wasn't for me.

"No, you don't. Far too infatuated with a woman's pussy, especially your *sweet girl*."

I froze. "You leave her out of this. Don't speak her fucking name."

The hood knocked back, and I stared into a skeletal face not so different than the mask in my pocket. Where this was plastic and other materials, his was made of sinew, bone, and a few vessels. Not fake but visceral, intimidating, and scary as fuck.

"Woah," I blurted, backing up.

"No need to do that. If I wanted you, I'd take you. If I intended harm, you would have experienced it already. Alas, I'm only here to broker a deal."

"What kind of deal?" I asked, instantly suspicious.

"It's more like a trade."

He shrugged, whipping off the robe and flicking it with his wrist, grinning when it flung toward me, snapped as it struck my chest, and slithered round my shoulders with a light hum. The vibration felt warm and soothing but also potent. Almost hypnotic.

I lifted my arms, blinking as the fiery fabric rolled across my body, almost like a caress. If I didn't know better, I would think this material was alive. Not in the way that humans live and breathe but in spiritual awareness, as if it was an entity with thoughts, feelings, and desires.

Creepy. Disturbing. Attractive.

"Who are you?"

He smiled as his face formed from shadow into a man's features. I wondered why he looked so familiar until I realized he favored a picture of my father in his youth when he was a new Marine fresh out of boot camp. I'd stared at the photo many times over the years, always proud of the man I called dad.

This wasn't my father.

"Who the hell are you?" I repeated, growing agitated.

The being snapped his fingers. "Lucifer Morningstar." He clicked his heels together as his body blinked, and he appeared in a dark gray suit, lavender-colored tie, and bright white pocket handkerchief. His polished shoes shined in the fading sunlight. Somehow, the day faded into night faster than time would typically allow.

Stars populated the sky as the orange ball disappeared beneath the horizon. The moon suddenly appeared, far too big and luminous. This was fucking weird.

"You loved the stars and moon as a child."

I did.

"You also loved to dissect things in school. Blood never scared you. Neither did the bones."

"What relevance does that have to anything?"

He winked. "I think you're an impressive addition to our club. You're the perfect skeletal warrior. A man wrapped in honor but unafraid to kill. Moral but easily corruptible. Intelligent but unafraid to be violent when the situation warrants."

Wonderful. The devil thought I was fun, contradictory, and a plaything. He could fuck right off with that.

I tried to pull off the robe, but it wouldn't budge. "I'm outta here."

"You shouldn't refuse my offer."

"Why not?"

"Because you can save Lacey."

I rushed him, pissed he spoke her name. "I said you don't say it. You don't think it. You don't go anywhere near my woman."

"You're savage." He shivered, grabbing his crotch as excitement danced in his dark eyes.

The fuck?

"I'm going to enjoy having you around."

"Back off," I warned as he grinned. Too wide.

Lucifer flicked his wrist, and a parchment shot out of his hand. I could see a contract with all the details spelled out, every way in which he owned the people who signed these documents. He provided protection in exchange for shadow warriors. Demonic entities that shared their power in exchange for human energy. A mutual symbiotic relationship. Both species benefitted, both thrived, and neither were harmed.

I would argue that demonic possession had its drawbacks.

Lucifer chuckled.

He could hear my thoughts, I finally realized.

"And if I decide I don't want this offer?"

Lucifer smiled. "Her life is fragile. I don't know."

"Don't patronize, manipulate, or lie to me."

Lucifer tilted his head, watching me. "Even I don't control everything. That is the truth. Refuse my help, and you have no guarantees. Accept, and you'll have a powerful ally."

"Let me see the contract."

He pushed it toward me, pacing as I read it, not worried, just bored. Lucifer already knew I would sign it. The crafty, sneaky bastard threw in a clause that ensured Lacey would survive as long as I bonded to a shadow warrior.

My shadow to be precise. Hand selected by Lucifer.

The dark entity would live inside me. He had secrets I couldn't access without agreeing to the contract and signing in my blood.

Fuck it. If I got to be with Lacey, this was worth it.

I picked off a scab on my wrist and swiped a finger through the fresh blood. Without hesitating, I signed my name, not a bit surprised when the blood sizzled on the paper, and all of it disappeared. The contract was binding now.

"We'll meet again, Skeletor. Enjoy your new shadows."

Shadows? I frowned, worried he deceived me.

Lucifer flicked me in the forehead, and I jolted, blinking as I focused on Manic, Creature, and Maddog. The devil had vanished.

"Fuck me," I growled. "Lucifer is a dick."

Manic snickered. Creature slapped me on the back.

Maddog ticked his chin my way. "You're one of us now. Get ready for the fuckening."

Yeah, I didn't like the sound of that.

Suddenly, I couldn't focus. A swirling mass of energy filled my body and seemed to take residence. My dick swelled, and I grew aroused, not for the men who stood around me, but for Lacey. I could smell her on me. Her musk and sweet pussy.

And I needed her. Now.

Across from me, my club brothers began laughing.

"There's the fuckening," Manic explained. "You'll have wood for days. Trust me, you need to fuck."

"As much as possible," Creature added.

For fuck's sake.

"Did you all go through this?"

Yeah, they did. I could tell it amused them to see me struggling with it. Assholes.

I guess I was on my way to Lacey. Hopefully, she wouldn't find it offensive when I rammed my cock inside her. I had a feeling I'd have her in bed for hours before I had enough. Maybe not even then.

Something powerful shifted inside me. I felt invincible.

Luis Diego was fucked.

ROYAL BASTARDS MC

Chapter 9

LACEY

THREE YEARS EARLIER

"Oh, God, Skel. You're bleeding!" We were attacked. Some guy I'd never seen before rushed toward us in the rain and stabbed Skel. In the parking lot. At a fucking Halloween party. "You're hurt."

He looked down, noticing the slash in his hoodie and the tee shirt underneath, watching as blood oozed from the wound. "Shit."

"What do you want me to do?" I asked, pulling out my phone. My hands shook as the adrenaline kicked in, and I blinked, trying hard to focus and not panic.

"Baby, it's not bad. Promise."

I finally found clarity and brushed my wet hair out of my face, trying to get a better look at the wound. "You need a hospital."

"No." He shook his head. "We just need to get to my place. I can take care of this myself."

"Skel, it's pouring rain, and you're losing blood."

"And I can handle a short ride home." He smirked. "Get on my damn bike, Sweet Girl. Stop draggin' this out."

I huffed as I sat on the wet leather seat, scrunching my face at the cold water seeping into my skin. This would be a horrible ride. I'd hate every minute.

But Skel was the one injured, not me. I could stop being a brat.

He sat in front of me, guiding my hands around his waist and positioning them so I pressed against his wound. His body stiffened as he breathed a harsh breath. "Fuck. Just apply pressure for me."

"I'll try."

He patted my hand. "You got this."

I should have been saying that to him.

The rain slowed as we merged onto the road, finally relenting as we rode toward his house. The wind had died down but still whipped our wet clothes around us. If it had been summer, I would have enjoyed the warm rain and the chill on my skin. In October? No.

My skin began to sting and burn. Skel trembled beneath my hands as we pulled to a stop at a red light. I couldn't imagine how difficult it must be to keep us safe on his bike while ignoring the pain in his side. Pressing against his back, I tried to give him some of my warmth.

"Such a good girl," he praised. "Keep holding tight, Lacey."

My arms ached, but it was nothing compared to what he endured. Warm blood coated my palm, and I worried he would lose too much. By the time we arrived at his place, both of us were exhausted. Skel parked in his garage and clicked the button to lower the door. He seemed stiff as I dropped my hands and stood.

I noticed the blood staining my fingers and bit my lip, worried when I saw him stand. "Let's get to your bathroom and the supplies."

He grunted as we entered his house, taking my hand as we walked through and stopped inside the bathroom. "Strip, Baby. We both need to get out of these wet clothes."

I nodded, wrestling with the French Maid costume and the clinging fabric, shivering as my cold fingers felt almost numb. Once I was naked, not even considering the option of hesitating, I watched as he turned on the shower.

Skel had one of those showers with all glass, and I followed him inside, gasping as the water hit my chilled skin. The waterfall showerhead was divine, dropping hot water on our shivering bodies. Heat from the steam fogged the glass as I sighed, staying under the spray to wet my hair until the dry, crusty feeling that had been left behind by the rain disappeared.

Skel leaned against the tile and pressed a hand to his side. "Come here."

I moved closer, dropping my head to look at the wound on his abdomen. His hand lifted.

"It's not that deep," he murmured.

"You're right, but it still looks awful. You've lost some blood."

"I can handle that. Had far worse overseas."

"As a Marine?" I clarified. He went twice if I remember correctly. Skel was a hero. *My* hero, too. I was already falling hard and fast for him. "I think you need stitches."

"Yeah. I do," he confirmed. "After we finish this shower."

"Does that mean I get to help wash you?" I asked with a wicked smile, trying hard not to stare at his crotch.

Skel's cock had lengthened, growing harder as he stared at me. "Anything you want, Sweet Girl. I'm yours."

Skel saved my life. Twice. He found me in that cemetery. He stopped the attacker from harming me and got injured in the process. He'd been there when I needed him since this started. The least I could do was show my gratitude.

I lowered to my knees, licking my lips as I stared up at him.

Skel's eyes were hooded. "Not gonna lie, Baby. You look damn good on your knees for me."

I reached for his erection, wrapping my hand around the base as I flicked my tongue toward the tip.

"Such a tease," he groaned.

Without warning, I took him in my mouth, nearly choking as I swallowed him down, stroking the hard length as he jolted.

"Damn." His hand slapped the tile while the other still pressed into his stomach. "Fuck. That feels good."

God, I was consumed by him. The feel of his cock like velvet but hard as steel. The taste of him was almost salty but unique. His scent clung to his skin. Woodsy and clean, with a hint of spice and remnants of leather and motor oil. It sounded odd, but I loved the combination.

My strokes increased in pace as I continued to bob my head, curling my tongue around his length, sucking, licking, and moaning because I couldn't get enough of him. I pumped his shaft as I squeezed, and he began to piston his hips.

I could tell it excited him. His hips rocked toward my face as I picked up the pace, eager to please him. I gagged several times but didn't stop. He touched the back of my throat as saliva dripped from my chin. Need pulsed between my thighs.

This turned me on too.

"I'm gonna come," he warned.

"Good," I managed to say with a mouth full of his dick.

"Where?" he growled, clenching his hand as if he fought to reach for me.

I pointed to my mouth, and he snarled, fisting my hair as he pulled me up and down on his length. His hips punched toward me. Once. Twice. Three times, before he shuddered. His cock twitched between my lips before he spilled into my mouth, shooting down my throat as I eagerly swallowed.

He panted as he withdrew, leaning his head against the tile. "Lacey. Fuck."

"Not good enough?" I teased.

"Best I ever had," he growled. "You're so fucking perfect."

I rose as he reached for me, resting my head against his chest. "We need to take care of you."

"You already did."

I snorted. "Your wound, my sexy hero."

He shook his head. "I'm no hero."

"You are to me," I replied softly, kissing the underside of his jaw. "Come on."

He relented, but I knew we'd have sex again soon. I wanted him, and I wasn't afraid to admit it.

He reached for two towels after he shut off the water. We dried off and dressed. Skel gave me a sweatshirt and joggers from his dresser. The fabric was soft and carried his scent. We moved to the kitchen, where he gathered supplies.

I never saw anyone stitch themselves up. It wasn't something I wanted to watch again. Every time the needle threaded through Skel's skin, I winced. It must have been agony, and he showed no sign of distress or pain, just calmly tied off each stitch and moved to the next one.

"Are you sure you're not a superhero?"

He laughed. "No, Baby. Just a man."

"You seem so much more. Larger than life," I admitted with awe. "You take down criminals. Sew up your own wounds. Wear a mask and eliminate your enemies. A sex god."

He shook his head. "You're somethin' else, Sweet Girl. A fucking breath of fresh air. Just what these old bones need."

"You're not old."

He paused to stare into my eyes. "A lot older than you."

"I don't care about that."

"You might when I'm old and gray, and you're still young and beautiful."

"Skel." It sounded like he was trying to convince me that we would never work. He should have thought about that before he fucked me. More than once. Or called me sweet girl. Or showed up and made me fall for him.

"Your father won't allow it."

So? "I'm an adult, Skel."

"But you're under his roof."

"What if I lived under yours?"

He frowned. "You ever live with a guy before? Or anywhere with a roommate?"

No. I sighed. "That doesn't mean I'm not capable of handling it."

"And what if ten years from now, you want a family, and I can't give you one?" Pain leaked through to strain his features before it vanished.

I didn't reply. I froze. Was he unable to have kids? Did it matter to me? I wasn't sure.

"And that's the deal breaker right there."

Skel returned to his stitches, bandaged the wound, and cleaned up. We didn't speak until he tugged a shirt over his head. "I'm taking you home."

I felt defeated. He'd shut me out. It was subtle, but I could still sense it. "I want to talk about this."

"We will."

Good.

"But your father needs to know what happened tonight."

I didn't argue as Skel led me to the garage. He didn't move to his Harley but brought me to his truck instead. We didn't say much on the ride to my building. Both of us were lost in our heads. We let that conversation about having kids rule us, and instead of dealing with it, we retreated.

Skel pulled in front of the high rise and parked by the doors, idling his truck. He didn't shut off the engine.

"You're not coming in?"

"No."

I didn't know why that hurt so much. He'd been there the whole time—a rock for me to lean on. And now, because of some minor issue, we couldn't seem to discuss, he was pulling away. "I would feel better if you did."

He seemed to think on it. "The judge is going to be upset, rightfully so, and I don't think my presence is wanted."

"It's wanted by me."

"Lacey."

"Come inside with me, Bran. I'm asking."

"I know it seems harsh, but I've got to say no."

Unbuckling my belt, I slid from the seat and opened the door, running from Skel because I couldn't believe he was acting like this. I never thought he'd stop fighting. He'd been an unmoving force of nature, a warrior, and a bodyguard. Nothing seemed to faze him. He faced every obstacle and quickly conquered it. Movies and songs were written about men like him. Strong. Brave. Everything. He was *everything* to me.

My heart broke as I realized what we shared had been far too brief but just enough to ruin me for anyone else. I wanted my Skel. My masked vigilante.

Maybe I was a silly girl who fell in love too fast. It was a character flaw that I clung to the people I cared about and held on too tight. After my mother died of cancer, it seemed to intensify. That was my shit to deal with, but it didn't mean that what I had with Skel wasn't real. I just wished he wanted me enough to push beyond his baggage and his past.

There was so much we needed to learn about each other. It was new. We'd barely begun to form an attachment. But it had taken root fast, burrowed deep, and I didn't think I could ever dig him out of my heart.

The building was quiet as I rushed inside. I ignored James as I walked to the elevator, too deep in my thoughts to notice much around me. The penthouse elevator lifted me high into the building, sliding open as I gasped.

Two men in black suits held guns pointed at my chest.

"I'm so glad you could join us," Luis Diego announced as he stood inside my door. "Your father is waiting."

Skel! I need you!

ROYAL BASTARDS MC

Chapter 10

SKEL

THREE YEARS EARLIER

My palm hit the steering wheel. Twice.

Frustration warred with the logical side of my brain. Lacey was too young. The age gap between us was too wide.

But it didn't feel that way when we were together. She was sweet and innocent in many ways but also sexy, determined, and courageous. Her maturity made her seem older, closer to her late twenties than younger.

I'd never met anyone like her. She brought out a wild, carnal side to me but also a tenderness that I'd never felt with another soul since my mother's death. What were the odds that Lacey would lose her mother the same way I lost mine, to the same cancer? It was tragic. Heartbreaking. And we both understood that helpless feeling that came along with it.

I couldn't put her through more heartache. It wouldn't happen tomorrow or even next year, but she'd want a family at some point, and I couldn't give her one.

Lifting my head, I glanced at her building before pulling away, knowing I wouldn't set foot inside again. Pissed that I was forced into making this decision when I just wanted to say fuck it and run to her made me feel edgy and tense.

I'm already falling in love with her.

I hadn't formed that thought yet. I hadn't put it into words, but that was the truth. I fucking loved this fierce, stunning woman, and I wanted to be with her. It didn't make sense. I never formed feelings for a woman this fast. But Lacey changed all the rules.

James moved in front of the door and stared at me. Something about the way he remained still, his eyes wide, immediately alerted me. He seemed scared. I ticked my chin at him and put my truck in drive, pulling away to park a short distance away from the building by the park. If anyone watched, they'd think I left.

My military upbringing and twenty years of service always trained me to have a weapon. I had all the legal paperwork to go with it and didn't give a fuck what anyone had to say about it, including the police. It was my fucking right to carry a gun. I knew how to use it with more skill than most people would ever learn.

I approached Lacey's building with caution, taking in my surroundings but finding nothing out of place. James let me in, and I noticed his stiff movements. "I'm taking the elevator up to the penthouse."

He nodded. "Careful."

The fact that he didn't say more, bouncing his gaze toward the security camera, convinced me that trouble awaited me in the penthouse. Someone went after the judge.

Fuck! I sent Lacey up there alone, distraught, and without a way to defend herself.

If anyone harmed her, I'd lose my shit.

I pushed the button on the elevator, unsurprised when the doors opened, and two men in black suits stared me down. "Looks like we're going to the same place," I observed, entering as the doors slid shut.

I probably could have let them subdue me. It might have been fun to let them think they got the upper hand before I smashed both of their faces into the walls, busting noses and knocking them out. I swear I considered it. But violence had taken root inside me the moment I realized Lacey was in danger.

Touch my woman, enter her house, threaten her, or make her cry, you're gonna regret it.

I knew the second those doors closed, the two goons would be on me. I ducked as they swung, colliding with one another as I kicked, swiping their feet out from under them. The first guy smacked his head into the wall hard enough to hear the crack.

The second guy rushed me. His head rammed into my stomach as I lifted my elbow and landed hard in the center of his back. His body sprawled across the floor of the elevator as I shoved my boot into his ass. He slammed into the wall headfirst and slumped down.

Good. Two assholes down. That made it easier.

I took their weapons, shoving the guns behind my back and into the waistband of my jeans. When they arrived at the bottom, James would see them. Hopefully, he'd call the police if he hadn't already.

I stepped out of the elevator as it opened, palming my weapon. Lights flickered in the hall from where someone had shot up the camera, light fixtures, and the black marble floor. Bits of crystal from the chandeliers spilled across the black marble and reflected prisms. Luckily enough, the windows weren't broken. That would have been hazardous, considering the penthouse was located on the thirty-fifth floor.

I moved as silently as possible, entering the penthouse with my gun raised. I wasn't stupid enough to think there wouldn't be more hitmen waiting inside. The kitchen was clear, but in the living room, sitting calmly on the sofa with his arms draped across the back, was Luis Diego. Three men stood behind the couch in identical dark suits—copies of their richer, more influential, and successful leader.

Judge Maxwell was tied up, his hands and feet bound. A cloth had been shoved in his mouth, and he couldn't speak. They positioned him on a chair as one of Luis's men kept a gun aimed at his chest.

Lacey gasped when she saw me. She perched on the edge of the sofa as far from Luis Diego as possible. She trembled, and I hated that she had to walk in here alone. Lacey never should have had to confront her kidnapper like that. I had to own that I failed her, and it pissed me off. She deserved better.

Guilt flooded me, but I winked at her before turning my attention to Luis. "Diego."

"Michael Brandon Myers. Gunnery Sergeant. Decorated hero. You've got quite a list of accomplishments, *amigo*."

"You forgot expert marksman and a black belt in MCMAP." I entered the room with my gun aimed at Luis, and I kept it there. "Neither of us needs to play games. I'll win."

Yeah, I was a cocky fucker, but I had the skills to back it up.

Luis chuckled. "I like you. Too bad I have to kill you."

His threat didn't mean shit to me. "It'll be the last mistake you ever make."

I knew what would happen next. Before his men could open fire, I tapped the trigger on my gun, hitting all three in quick succession, so fast only one of them had a chance to fire a shot, and it hit the wall behind me. All three bodies fell.

"Should we try this again, *friend*?"

Luis grinned, but it didn't reach his eyes. "What do you want? The girl? Take her."

"And the judge?"

"He owes me a favor. I'm hoping to influence him with a little motivation."

I didn't like the sound of that. "The police are already on their way."

"Yes, I know. Clever, aren't you?"

This was too easy. Luis was far too relaxed.

"Skel!" Lacey shouted as I heard someone behind me.

I should have checked more thoroughly before I allowed my back to be vulnerable. Of course, I didn't have much choice when I walked in. I had to ensure Lacey was safe. She was my first priority. The judge came second. If I had to choose one life, it would be hers every time.

The person behind me made the mistake of hesitating. That was their downfall. I spun and pushed out the palm of my hand, chopping at the guy's throat. I knew I hit hard enough to break his windpipe when he gasped and fell to the ground, clutching at his throat. I didn't stick around to find out if he was suffocating. I didn't care.

The room exploded into action. Lacey raced to her father. Luis rushed me. The guy on the floor kicked his feet as death took him.

I heard someone else enter the penthouse.

"Police!"

Luis and I collided. His body hit mine, and we rolled on the ground. I punched the side of his head as he jabbed at my side. His plan backfired because he never counted on me. He thought he could intimidate the judge and use Lacey to force his hand. But I showed up and interrupted him.

I'd made an enemy of Luis Diego before I ever met him simply because I helped Lacey that night in the cemetery.

Luis pulled a knife from his pocket and slashed, nearly slicing off my ear. We struggled as more shouting followed—orders from the police. Luis wouldn't relent. A bullet shot through his hand as he screamed, dropping the knife.

I kicked it away as I stood, concerned for Lacey.

"Skel!" Tears tracked down her face as she struggled to get her father's bound limbs untied.

The judge cursed Luis Diego as one of the officers approached him, asking what happened. "He invaded my home and threatened me and my daughter. I want him arrested! Now!"

The judge was nearly hysterical. It took Lacey a minute to calm him enough to speak without shouting.

He turned to me, and the hostility in his gaze surprised me. I just saved his life and his daughter and helped subdue his enemy. A little gratitude would be nice.

He shook his head. "Never," he whispered.

I knew what that meant. He'd never be okay with me in Lacey's life. I wouldn't be working for him. He didn't want me around. The judge would do everything he could to keep us apart.

Lacey was an adult. She could do what she wanted. Still, I hated that it would complicate things with her father. He was all she had.

She left the judge's side as he began making a statement. Her teeth nibbled on her bottom lip. "Thank you."

"Anytime, Lacey."

Luis was taken into custody. We watched as officers led him to the elevator. He struggled, trying to fight the handcuffs slapped onto his wrists. He threatened everyone as the doors closed.

I didn't have a doubt that he'd see the inside of a jail cell after this. Lacey and the judge were safe. The nightmare was over.

"It's over," she breathed with a sigh of relief. "I'm so grateful for your help. Who knows what would have happened if you didn't come back?"

I didn't want to think about it.

She cleared her throat. "Why did you? Come back, I mean."

Lacey looked nervous, fidgeting with the old fraying hem of the sweatshirt I'd given her after we showered together at my place. She looked fucking good in my clothes. Too good.

It didn't change anything from the conversation we'd had before I dropped her off. I still couldn't have children. She would want a family. Loving each other wouldn't be enough someday. I was a pragmatist. Ending it now would hurt a hell of a lot less than five or ten years down the line.

"I had to be sure you were okay."

"Well," she shrugged, "I don't think I am." I caught the glassy shine of tears before she blinked them back. Her hands clenched before she rested her palms against her thighs. Nervous energy radiated from her.

She knew what came next.

"But you will be. I'm certain of that." I pulled her into my arms for a hug, needing that last bit of contact with her before I said the words that would cut off any chance of us being together. "You take care of yourself and the judge."

She tensed as I released her. "That's it?"

Fuck. The gutted expression on her face tore me apart inside.

"I'm leaving Vegas, Lacey. I won't be coming back."

She smacked me, and I didn't flinch. Just let her hit me several times as a sob broke loose from her chest. Tears pooled in her pretty eyes before she turned away, refusing to let them fall in my presence.

I was a dick. I owned it.

But she didn't know I felt every bit of her heartache, and it added to my own.

ROYAL BASTARDS MC

Chapter 11

SKEL

PRESENT

NOTHING WORKED OUT LIKE it was supposed to. I told Lacey I'd be back to talk to her father, but I never got a chance. The little ride into the desert changed everything. First, I was horny as fuck. I couldn't wait to get to my woman. Second, the knowledge that Manic and Creature had picked up the asshole who invaded my home surged a new need through my body. *Vengeance.*

My cock throbbed for Lacey. My head refused to allow me to leave until I found out how the intruder knew where I lived and why the fuck he arrived with his buddies after I brought Lacey home. I'd been watched. That much was obvious.

But who? Why? This felt far more complicated than Luis Diego and a little revenge. Sure, he was probably still pissed when I showed up and ruined his plans, interrupting when he went after the judge and Lacey three years ago.

Still, I didn't buy there wasn't another motive.

This stunk like club retribution, and the only club we had an issue with in Las Vegas and Tonopah were the fucking Bladed Serpents MC. The Tonopah chapter eliminated all others.

I puffed on my cigarette as I leaned against the building, needing that shot of nicotine before I took my turn on the prisoner. I let Manic and Creature work him over first. He needed to be worn down, bloodied, and broken when I went downstairs. If he wasn't? I would finish the job.

No matter what, I was getting answers. I had to protect my woman. Lacey was gonna be my ol' lady. All that shit that kept us apart? We could work through it.

And the family part? I would figure out a way to make her happy. We could adopt. Look into other ways for her to conceive. I didn't give a fuck as long as we stayed together. If she wanted babies, I would give them to her. Anything she wanted.

I flicked the last of my cigarette to the ground, stomping out the cinders, and headed back inside the clubhouse. Maddog spotted me and gestured for me to join him at the bar.

"We haven't learned anything useful. I'm thinkin' the asshole down there is savin' all the juicy shit for you."

That thought occurred to me, too. It made sense. He came to my house. "I'm going down now."

There was a massive cellar in this old casino. It had been used for storage in the last couple of decades, but now that we gutted it and placed tool benches and weapon racks down here, it resembled a torture chamber. Chains and hooks were poking out of bins that lined the walls. We even bought a blacksmith forge.

The point was that we had a place to work. And if that included interrogating anyone threatening the club, so be it.

I didn't waste time being polite when I reached the bottom of the stairs. Manic and Creature had strapped our prisoner to a metal embalming table. His wrists and ankles were pulled tight at the four corners, which left him vulnerable. His clothes had been stripped from his body. Nothing made a man feel more exposed than his naked flesh on display.

I picked up pliers and walked to his side. "Why did you come to my house?"

Silence.

I clamped his nipple and twisted, pulling hard on his skin.

The prisoner howled.

"Why did you come to my house?" I twisted more, ripping off part of his nipple.

"Fuck! Stop!"

"Answer me, motherfucker, or I will rip your body apart one piece at a time. I'm not as patient as they are," I informed him, gesturing to Manic and Creature.

"Ratchet," he blubbered through tears. "He's at the core of all of it. I'll tell you everything. I never wanted this shit."

Why didn't he cooperate before now? "Why didn't you say anything sooner?"

"I was waiting to tell *you*."

Yeah, I thought so. "Why me?"

"Ratchet wants to tear down this club before it can get started. He's lookin' to expand his territory, but the reason he started with you is because of Luis Diego. He paid Ratchet and the club."

"For?" I asked, already knowing the answer.

"The judge, his daughter, and the shit from three years ago. He's fucking obsessed with making you all suffer."

And there it was. Luis Diego sought help as soon as he was released from prison. He'd hooked up with old friends and made alliances with new ones. Ratchet didn't pass up the opportunity to make a buck or hurt the RBMC.

"There's something else."

"What?" I asked, hoping this didn't have anything to do with Lacey.

Something stirred inside me—a feeling of rage that wasn't my own. I felt my body temperature rise and the presence of an entity. He moved within shadows, forming in my mind.

No skin, no physical body, but I saw a skeletal face. Red glowing eyes.

And I heard a deep, scratchy voice.

We must protect Lacey.

The thought wasn't my own.

I startled, focusing on the prisoner on the table. "Tell me."

"Luis Diego will be at The Naked Slipper tonight."

I hated that name. We needed to rename the strip club asap.

This was the information I needed. Finally, I could take down that asshole. He shouldn't have survived after what he did to Lacey.

Touch our woman and die.

Power flowed through my blood. I felt the creature in my veins. He slithered through every part of me. Instead of feeling creeped out, I felt the power inside me intensify.

"Check it out," Maddog ordered. I wasn't sure how long he'd been there or listened in. "Bring Creature and Manic."

The shadows swirled inside me. I felt their presence burst from my skin and hover around my body. I turned to the guy on the table, hating he was a rat.

"Boo, motherfucker," I growled, feeling my shadows pulse with amusement as the prisoner pissed himself.

Maybe bonding with a demonic being had its privileges.

Skel.

Lacey's voice popped into my head. Shit. She needed me.

WE WALKED TO THE strip club instead of riding our bikes. It wasn't far, and we owned most of this street. Time to make our presence felt and kick some ass.

I had a plan and discussed it with my brothers before we entered The Naked Slipper. It probably would have gone down the right way if I hadn't walked inside and found my girl on the center stage. She strutted as she made her way to the pole, swishing her ass with every step.

Music pumped through the speakers. Stuck in place, I couldn't seem to move.

Lacey wore a schoolgirl uniform, and the striptease had every fucker in this place hot for her. Pieces of her costume flung outward as she tossed them in all directions. The way she moved her body to the song she chose had me throbbing with need. When she got down to her panties and a lacey bra, far too enticing in virginal white, I nearly stomped onstage. But something inside prevented me from moving.

"Hey," I whispered, knowing my shadow was responsible.

Watch.

Lacey's hands wrapped around the pole as she reached it, and she kicked up her legs, swinging around as her ass and those long, sexy, smooth legs sent her through the air in a sensual spin. She worked that pole like she'd been born to it. I never saw a woman at ease quite like it, thrusting her satin-clad pussy toward the metal as she gyrated.

Fuck. Me.

We need to buy her one.

Hell yeah, we did.

Blonde hair and sensual curves had me engrossed. The whole place could have burned down, and I wouldn't have noticed.

She had my complete and undivided attention. When she noticed I was there, staring at her, Lacey licked her lips and smiled.

She was fucking beautiful. Sky-blue eyes almost too innocent and big for her face. Curves and a juicy ass. Those sexy legs that wrapped around me on my bike.

Fuck. I wanted her. Now. Tomorrow. *Forever.*

Lacey had a combination of sweet innocence and sensual grace that did wicked things to my brain and body. My cock tingled whenever I looked at her. She aroused my dick, my curiosity, and the desire to learn more about her. Everything we never got a chance to talk about three years ago. I wanted it all with her.

Seeing her here only strengthened my resolve. I had to make her my ol' lady. She was a morally sweet girl in a house of corruption. A little vixen who walked on the wild side. All I could ever need or desire.

Her stare caressed me from head to boots as she continued to rock her hips and sway her ass to the beat. When the song ended, she blew a kiss into the crowd, but her stare had locked on me.

All fucking mine.

Ours.

Yes. Ours.

Creature stood beside me. "Diego is here."

He came for her performance.

Fuck. I bet that asshole did.

"Let's end this."

Creature nodded, and Manic joined us, heading toward the back of the club and a hall that led to private rooms. A security guard tried to stop us, but Manic pulled him aside. I didn't wait to notice if he had to use force or not. Blood would spill tonight. I knew that for certain.

This was our club now. We made the rules, and the hostile takeover was just beginning.

I spotted Luis Diego as he entered one of the rooms. He had to have seen Lacey. Maybe he enjoyed the show. Or perhaps he would order her to join him. I didn't know how it would go down. Didn't matter. Whatever he started, I'd finish.

We pulled our guns as we reached the room, busting inside, weapons drawn. Diego was expecting us. No surprise there. Several of his men flanked him.

But the other man in the room wasn't expected. He wore a cut with the serpent and blade patch. President adhered to the front along with his name: Ratchet.

Creature moved closer. He had waited a long time to find out who ordered the hit on his mother. Years for retribution and the truth. Now, he finally had a chance to learn if Ratchet was behind all of it.

This had come together a little too easily. Maybe it was fate.

Ratchet had stayed on with the club after Tinman left. The asshole had to know what went down with the hit and who ordered it. Tinman's wife's murder was too much. He had a son to raise and didn't want that life to take away anyone he loved. He broke all ties with the Bladed Serpents MC.

But Creature never let it go. He couldn't.

"Ah, Tinman's son. You look just like him. Well, without the wheelchair."

That was fucked.

Creature took a step in Ratchet's direction and snarled. "You order the hit on my mother?"

"Yeah, boy, I did. What are you gonna do about it?"

Several things happened at once.

One of the Bladed Serpents MC members entered the room and shoved Lacey into it. Creature lost his shit. Manic watched his back, aiming his gun at the BSMC members.

And me? I let my shadows out to play.

ROYAL BASTARDS MC

Chapter 12

LACEY

PRESENT

I WAS SO CONFUSED. Why were the Bladed Serpents MC at the strip club when the Royal Bastards MC owned the bar? Skel mentioned that ownership changed hands, which meant the old owners had to vacate.

What was happening?

I got shoved into a room by one of the Serpents after my performance on stage. I'd done it as a distraction since the detective I worked with on the case asked for my help. Skel was going to be pissed. At least, I thought so until his hungry gaze watched me work the pole, and he didn't hide the growing bulge between his legs as a result of it.

Turning my man on? An added bonus.

I knew the police had finished gathering intel on Ratchet, the Bladed Serpents, Luis Diego, and Angel Mackenzie. They were all going to prison for a long time.

Skel stiffened as soon as he saw me. His jaw locked.

Everyone in the room was tense. I didn't focus on the others, only caring about my biker—the guy who was going to put a ring on my finger. Even if he hadn't asked me yet. And maybe, I'd get to be an ol' lady.

I looked up what it meant. I'd be his property, but that was a biker's way of laying claim. An ol' lady was protected, loved, cherished, and respected. What more could a woman want? Oh, fantastic sex. I had that in spades.

My guy knew how to fuck me right. No complaints there.

I wasn't paying attention, and that proved to be a mistake when the room erupted in chaos. Guns were drawn. People began shouting. Some threatened others.

My hair was yanked, and my head snapped back. Shocked, I tried to twist out of the grasp. "Hey!"

"Don't move, *princesa*."

Shit! Luis Diego dragged me across the room as I flailed, trying to hit him but failing. He kept me turned enough that I couldn't make contact with any body parts. A shame. I'd love to stomp all over his flaccid dick.

"Let me go!"

"Take your hands off her," Skel demanded.

"You've caused enough trouble, Skeleton Man. Time you learned who's in charge."

Skeleton Man. My masked vigilante.

I managed to turn enough to see him. There was no mask tonight. No face paint.

But . . .shadows began to seep from Skel. They grew in intensity, taking shape and forming a thick, heavy mass. Inside the dark cloud, I saw *faces*.

Multiple skeletal images overlapped and grinned. The deep, sinister laughter that followed was horrifying, but somehow, I sensed it was only a threat to Luis. I felt protected by the mass.

So weird.

"Let her go," Skel ordered one final time.

Luis Diego seemed hypnotized. He watched the skeletal images floating in the shadows and whimpered. His hand finally released me, and I winced at the ache in my scalp.

"Lacey. Come here."

I rushed to Skel as he slid an arm around me. The shadows began to pulse and writhe, flowing around my limbs and body. I felt caressed. Desired. And turned on. Holy shit. My core ached, and my clit pulsed with need. Lust filled the red eyes of the phantom faces. They wanted me. Wow.

"Uh, Skel?"

Sure. I had a mask kink. That was obvious by now. Same with sex in the open where I could get caught. Another kink.

But ghostly faces and shadows? That was something new. I didn't know how I felt about it.

"You're protected, my Sweet Girl. Nothing and no one will harm you. You're mine. All of me."

Um, okay. Kinda hard not to feel special after that.

But wait. How would that work? Did the shadows play?

Soft touches brushed across my skin, and my nipples hardened. I felt a light caress on my inner thigh and then a tickle against my clit. I jolted. Instant arousal flooded my body, and I had to hold back a moan.

A girl could get used to having foreplay like this.

Skel growled, and I realized I had missed what was happening around me. The shadows used their skills to distract me. I might have protested, but it felt good, and I didn't have to deal with Luis Diego.

Awareness slowly brought clarity. It was strange. Like the shadows had kept me hidden within them while a battle raged in the room. A haze of protection that kept me safe. No one could touch me but Skel and the shadows.

As that veil lowered and I saw all the bodies, I gasped.

"It's okay, Lacey. Had to be done, Sweet Girl." Skel held me against his chest, wrapping me in his embrace. "He won't ever come after you or the judge again."

Relief swept through me. I thought it was handled when Luis went to prison, but that only enraged him. He would never stop. I knew that now. Skel had to end it.

I closed my eyes tight, not wanting to see the blood and carnage. Justice had been served on multiple levels tonight. I could tell from the shift in the room. There was a peace I felt that wasn't there when I first walked in here.

How strange that I could sense it.

"It's the shadows," Skel whispered. "They're communicating with you. I feel it."

"The feds are outside."

I opened my eyes, staring at the biker Skel called Creature. He was intense.

"We need to finish up here."

"The bodies," Skel replied.

"I know, brother."

"You got closure, Creature. Happy for you, brother."

"And you got your ol' lady."

Skel held me tighter.

"Someone call for a cleanup?"

The three of us turned at the sound of the cheerful voice, staring at the door. Two men I'd never met but wore Royal Bastards leather vests joined us. I caught the names on their patches: Diablo and Rael.

Rael startled me when I saw his face. He wore Day of the Dead-themed makeup with black and white and skeletal features. It was far different than Skel's mask or his shadows.

Diablo wore red and black face paint. He grinned at Skel, and I shivered. It was so demonic that I was glad I had Skel with me.

Both bikers were intimidating, but something different hovered over them. A feeling that they were warriors and protectors, like Skel. Enhanced. Powerful. Almost like the hand of death.

"Reapers," Skel whispered.

Woah. Actual grim reapers?

Uh, we needed to leave. They harvested souls!

As if they all heard my thoughts, dark laughter followed.

Skel steered me toward the door. "Let's go, my little vixen. I've got a surprise for you."

"Okay." I didn't want to stick around anyway.

Outside, Skel led me down the sidewalk, clenching my hand. Blue and red lights flashed in the darkness, but the police weren't arresting anyone. I guessed the other bikers would handle it.

We stopped at a gate, and a young guy opened it. Skel led me through, gesturing toward the parking lot and the row of motorcycles parked outside the massive building.

"This is home, Lacey."

I swallowed hard, afraid to ask for clarity.

He tilted my chin up, hovering his mouth above mine. "Your home and mine. It's the new clubhouse. Doesn't matter where we end up, though, Baby. Just stay with me. I fucking love you, Lacey."

My heart soared.

Nothing had ever sounded more perfect.

ROYAL BASTARDS MC

Chapter 13

SKEL

PRESENT

I ROLLED TO A stop outside the cemetery, shutting down the engine on my bike. When I stood, Lacey followed, removing her helmet. I stored it in the saddlebags and turned toward her, ticking my head toward the rows of headstones, the light fog playfully rolling across to disguise the ground, and the moon crawling its way up the night sky.

She didn't have a clue what I planned for her.

"Run," I ordered, removing my mask from my cut and pulling it on.

She tilted her head, confused. "What?"

It probably didn't make sense to her. But I'd found her in a cemetery and I wanted to make her come in one.

She shouldn't fear the shadows because I owned them. At dawn, I would ask her to marry me. It was perfect.

Until then, I would hunt her all night among the headstones and fog. I'd fuck her every time I caught her. A catch and release, cat and mouse type of game. I wanted her pumped full of my cum and leaking it all over the cemetery grounds.

Our story began here. It would continue here too.

Time to play, Sweet Girl.

"Run, my sweet little temptress. But know when I find you, I'll be fucking you."

She blinked, knocking her knees together as her thighs clenched. My woman loved sex in public places, and she grew insatiable when I fucked while wearing my skeleton mask.

"That's right. I'm going to shove my cock deep inside you, Lacey. I might even let my shadows play."

Her eyes widened. She loved the idea of it.

"But it's not gonna be once. I'm hunting you all night until dawn."

That seemed to do it.

Lacey's lips parted. The idea intrigued her.

Without another word, she sprinted away from me, rushing through the gate and the fog, which created waves of cool mist, pulsing as it reformed in her absence.

This is going to be fun.

The shadows hovered around my shoulders as I counted in my head. They waited for my instructions, eager to hunt. I could feel their desire and excitement. My cock hardened, and I pressed against my jeans, feeling the rough material dig into my bare skin.

I'd gone commando tonight. Nothing would stop me from claiming Lacey. The less in the way, the better. I couldn't wait to bend her over a headstone or push her up against a crypt wall. There were so many intriguing places to fuck her in a cemetery.

We'll have her screaming for us.

Yes. Screaming. Coming. Dripping.

When I reached one hundred, I headed in the direction she ran. The silent graves added to the spooky atmosphere as I began to listen, hoping I could catch her footfalls or breathing. The wind was almost nonexistent, and the trees barely moved. Any chill came from the low temperature alone.

It took several minutes as I stalked through the rows, pausing to listen for any hint of Lacey's movements. I heard leaves crinkle to my right and turned, following the noise as it continued. She wasn't trying hard to stay quiet. Hadn't anyone ever taught her how to be suitable prey?

I smirked as I caught her shadow. It swept over a nearby headstone, and I approached, slowing my steps.

"Skel," she called. "I'm naked, and I'm playing with my pussy."

Naughty girl.

We'd have to try this again. Once she had proper instructions, we could drag this out much longer.

Right now? I just wanted to bury my cock inside her and feel her warmth clench around me.

I found Lacey bending over a grave. Her ass jutted out, and she wore nothing to hide her bare pussy or the slick glistening on her fingers as she strummed her clit.

"Oh, God, Skel. I need you."

I see that, Sweet Girl.

"Put your hands on the grave and widen your legs."

She obeyed, removing her fingers as she moaned. Her ass jiggled as she taunted me. "Skel."

I unsnapped my jeans and stepped behind her, yanking down my zipper. My cock sprang free, eager to be inside Lacey. "You'll take my dick, Baby. Every hard inch. And I want you to scream when you come. Wake the fucking dead with that orgasm. You hear me?"

She did.

I gave her no warning before I slammed inside her tight, wet heat, holding onto her hips as I began to pump hard. Her cries seemed to echo in the stillness. Just the idea that we were fucking like this sent a thrill through me.

The slapping of our flesh could be heard as we rutted against each other, driving our need higher. I could feel the arousal building and us both heading toward a wild release.

Knowing it would send her over the edge, I let the shadows hold onto her wrists and ankles, spreading her wide as I fucked her. A shiver ghosted my spine as dark, sultry laughter filled my head.

Yes, let's fuck her. Hard.

And I did. More than once. All fucking night.

We didn't leave that cemetery until close to dawn.

And guess what? She said yes.

I hope you enjoyed Skeletor and Lacey's story.

Maddog's story is available now in *Hell on Wheels*, the first book in the Las Vegas, NV RBMC.

You can read more about Manic in *Reckless Mayhem*.

Creature's story is *Jeepers Creepers*.

Watch for more RBMC Las Vegas, NV coming soon!

If you're new to the Tonopah, NV Royal Bastards MC, start with *The Biker's Gift* or you can skip the first two novellas and dive into the series with *Ridin' for Hell* and *Devil's Ride*.

Find all Nikki's Royal Bastards MC books on Amazon and Kindle Unlimited.

Never miss out on a book! Follow Nikki on social media to receive updates.

LAS VEGAS, NV CHAPTER

Pres – Maddog

V.P. – Skeletor

SGT at Arms – Manic

Enforcer – Creature

Nomad/Enforcer – Darius "The Jackal"

Secretary – Crusher

Treasurer – Dice

Road Captain – Hex

Tail Gunner – Slash

Member/Cleaner – Tombstone

Member/Tech – Snapshot

Chaplain – Testament

Royal Bastards MC Las Vegas, NV

#1 Hell on Wheels

#2 Reckless Mayhem (Manic Parts 1 & 2)

#3 Jeepers Creepers

#4 Rattlin' Bones

Mayhem Makers: Manic Mayhem (Manic Part 1)

TONOPAH, NV CHAPTER

Pres/Founder – Grim Reaper

VP/Founder – Mammoth

SGT at Arms – Azrael, Angel of Death "Rael"

Enforcer – Exorcist

Enforcer – Jigsaw

Secretary – Wraith

Treasurer – Hannibal

Road Captain – Patriot

Tail Gunner – Chaos

Founder – Papa

Member – Chrome

Member – Bodie

Member – Bones

Member/Cleaner – Diablo

Member/Tech – Xenon

Member – Shadow

Member – Toad

Member – Spook

Prospect – Zane

Playlist

When the Darkness Comes – Jeris Johnson

Bite Down – Mike's Dead

Evil People – Set It Off

Gone or Staying – Sleep Theory

I Got Mine – The Black Keys

Fall Eternal – Black Veil Brides

Rain – Sleep Token

Werewolf – Motionless In White

Thriller – No Resolve & From Ashes to New

Blackout – Versus Me

Shackles – Steven Rodriguez

Porn Star Dancing (feat. Zakk Wylde) – My Darkest Days

Monster in Me – From Ashes to New

The Summoning – Sleep Token

RATATATA – BABYMETAL & Electric Callboy

Skeleton – Set It Off

You can listen to Nikki's Playlists on Spotify.

One Hell of a ride!

Royal Bastards MC, founded in 2019.

Royal Bastards MC Facebook Group -
https://www.facebook.com/groups/royalbastardsmc/

Website - https://www.royalbastardsmc.com/

Love to read romance?

Check out these books by Nikki Landis:

Devil's Murder MC

#1 Crow

#2 Raven

#3 Hawk

#4 Talon

#5 Crow's Revenge

#6 Heron's Flame

#7 Cuckoo

#8 Claw

#9 Carrion

#10 TBD

Feral Rebels/RBMC Crossover

#1 Claimed by the Bikers

#2 One Night with the Bikers

#3 Snowed In with the Bikers

Reaper's Vale/RBMC Crossover

#1 Twisted Iron

#2 Savage Iron

Kings of Anarchy MC: Ohio

#1 Property of Scythe

#2 Property of Mountain

#3 TBD

Ravage Riders MC

#1 Sins of the Father

#2 Sinners & Saints

#3 Sin's Betrayal

#4 Life of Sin

#5 Born Sinner

Saint's Outlaws MC: Las Vegas, NV

Prequel: My Christmas Biker

#1 Brick's Redemption

#2 Dagger's Claim

Summit Hill Vipers

Mayhem Makers: My Inked Neighbor

#1 My Stepbrother Biker

#2 My Tattooed Hitchhiker

#3 My Ex-Boyfriend Stalker

#4 TBD

Summit Hill Asylum

#1 Don't Scream

#2 Say hush

#3 Just Bleed

Night Striders MC

#1 Rebel Road

#2 TBD

Iron Renegades MC

#1 Roulette Run

#2 Jester's Ride

#3 Surviving Saw

Ground Zero: Origins

Standalones

In the Wake of Death

The Devil Next Door

Unmasked

SNEAK PEEK

HERON'S FLAME

"**H**OW WAS THE DATE?" Hawk asked, dropping beside me in church.

Talon sat in the empty seat on my right. "You sure got back late."

How the fuck did they know what time I brought Rebel home? No one was awake.

"Not sure it's your business," I replied, kicking back in my seat. Crow wasn't here, but he would arrive and start church soon.

"Come on. Don't hold out on us," Hawk urged.

"I promised my ol' lady I'd ask," Talon added.

"Callie and Gail will probably talk to Rebel, so I don't have to say shit."

Hawk snorted. "Oh, they'll talk."

Yeah, I thought so.

"I just want to compare notes. See if we can find out more than them," Talon laughed.

I wasn't gonna say a damn thing now.

"You just ruined it, Talon," Hawk huffed.

"How do you know what time I got back?" I asked, too curious to drop it.

"Saw you pull in." Hawk shrugged. "I needed a smoke."

Ah. I didn't know how I missed him when I parked my bike. I must have been too wrapped up in Rebel to notice.

"I decided to let you have a few moments alone before I walked inside," Hawk added.

"How generous," I mumbled.

"Have you shown her your crow yet?" Talon turned toward me, grinning like he knew a secret I didn't. "It's not like it'll surprise her."

Shit. I forgot about the circumstances of Rebel's arrival. She came to The Roost after captivity on Undertaker's lands. I found out about Undertaker and the war with the Dirty Death MC after I patched into the club last month. I knew he was no longer a threat, or I'd go after him for kidnapping Rebel. The Tonopah Royal Bastards used their reapers to separate the vargulf and the Alpha wolf, sending the evil part straight to Lucifer in hell. I missed all that, but I'd heard about it numerous times.

A truce had formed after the reaping, and now Undertaker, or Alpha Caden, no longer posed a threat. His club had become allies with ours. In fact, the Dirty Death no longer existed. His club had voted on a new name: Night Striders MC.

Still, I didn't know if I could hold back if I saw him. He took Rebel, kept her locked in a dirty underground cell, and hurt her. I cracked my neck, instantly on edge.

"Brother," Talon began, clapping my shoulder. "It's the past. Let it go."

"Would you say that if it was Gail?" I asked, flipping it back on him.

Talon cringed.

"Yeah, I didn't think so."

"Crow's orders," Hawk interjected. "Hands off."

I nearly growled in response.

"Hey, I'm not sayin' I don't get it. Hell, I'd go after any motherfucker who tried to hurt Callie."

He understood. Good. "I don't know if I can let it go."

Hawk and Talon tensed.

"I'm not sayin' I'll go hunt down Undertaker on his land." Both nodded. "But if I see that fucker here, he's gonna have my boot up his ass."

Hawk chuckled.

Talon shook his head. "I can't say I blame you."

I had met Alpha Caden/Undertaker twice before I knew what he'd done to Rebel. A part of me felt that retribution was needed regardless of the circumstances. A truce didn't matter. He had to suffer for the wrongs he'd done. The crows outside begin to stir. Caws echoed as I heard the flapping of wings. I felt their agitation.

"What about your crow?" Hawk asked, keeping his voice low as the room filled with members.

I'd had several experiences with my crow—many more with the murder. I was still learning about our bond. My childhood and lack of knowledge left a gap in my growth. The bond occurred naturally, but my ability to control my shift still felt unstable.

I knew I had abilities similar to Hawk's. He could partially shift, sprout wings, and fly as one of them. Strange, but also fucking awesome. I needed to learn better control before I could master flight.

"I'm working on it."

Hawk nodded. "Hit me up if you need flight time."

Yeah, I would. Soon. But my focus shifted to Rebel, and nothing felt half as important as her. I heard the crows rattle their throats in agreement. They felt affection and urgency around Rebel. The need to protect her almost overrode common sense. She wasn't in danger, so I didn't understand why I kept feeling these strong emotions.

Nothing would harm her at The Roost.

"What's got you on alert?" Talon asked, noticing that I sat forward, staring at the door.

"Rebel. I can't shake the feeling that something isn't right. I feel I've got to be with her every hour of the day." It sounded crazy, possessive, and overprotective.

"Aw shit," Talon laughed.

Hawk grinned. "You're almost mated now."

Mated? I hadn't fucked Rebel yet. How was that possible?

Of course, I wasn't telling Hawk or Talon.

"When the crow knows." Talon ticked his head toward me. "That's it. There's no stopping it."

"Stopping what?" Crow wondered as he entered the chapel. He took his position at the head of the table and picked up the gavel. With a quick slam on the wooden surface, he brought the meeting to order. "Might as well tell us all, Heron."

I had the attention of everyone in the room. Fuck. "Me. Rebel is my mate."

The room erupted in chuckles and groans, money exchanging hands as those who lost forked over their cash and those who won snatched their earnings.

Motherfuckers. All of them.

"You're all assholes," I grumbled, crossing my arms over my chest. "Shouldn't you be happy for me instead of betting on whether or not I can seal the deal?"

Cuckoo snorted. "Don't get your panties twisted, Heron."

Crow held up a hand as the room silenced. "Our boy is finally growing up and popping his cherry."

After that, I decided to ignore every last one of them. Indefinitely.

The laughter took way too fucking long to die down.

"Heron, you're one of us. Get used to this shit. Just remember, when one of them goes through it, you get to return the favor."

Crow had a point.

"Back to business. We have a new player in town. A crew who's been pushing drugs through Vegas and close to our territory."

The room sobered; no hint of amusement remained.

Raven frowned. "They got a name?"

"Grave Robbers MC. New president, too. Goes by Hammerhead."

Hmmm. Something about that information didn't sit right. It wasn't just the name or how it reminded me of Rebel and our trip to the aquarium, but also the timing.

"We know his real name? Or what he wants?" I asked, feeling the tension build in my shoulders. That dangerous vibe and the overwhelming feeling I needed to protect Rebel grew stronger.

"No, but he's asked for a meet. I've decided it's best to sit down with him at the rally. It's neutral ground. If shit goes down, we got plenty of brothers to watch our backs."

Smart.

"And the Royal Bastards?" Hawk wondered.

"They'll be with us. We good with that?"

Fists pounded the table as the members agreed.

"Eagle Eye?" Crow rumbled as the man in question lifted his head. "Need you to dig up whatever you can find on Hammerhead and his club. I want to know his real name, the members, and anything else to give us an advantage before the rally."

"You got it, pres."

"Only officers at the meet, but I don't want anyone goin' far. You stay at the rally. No one leaves."

Nods from the men in the room followed.

"Until then, we celebrate Bella's birthday. She's looking forward to the barbecue tonight. I got all her favorite foods, and several deliveries are still being made. Stay sharp. I don't want any surprises with Hammerhead showing up in Las Vegas."

His concerns were legit. We didn't know shit about this guy, his club, or what they wanted. Until we did, we kept our shit locked down. Asking for a meeting this close to the rally roused suspicion, especially because it happened at the last minute.

After church, I spent several hours helping with deliveries and prep. A sweaty mess, I headed back to my room to shower, change clothes, and prepare for the party. When I shoved my arms through the sleeves of my cut, I noticed my phone had several missed texts.

Rebel missed me.

With a grin, I swiped across to read her messages when I caught the photo she sent me.

Oh, dirty girl. You're gonna pay for this, preferably with my hand on your ass.

"Or my cock in your pussy," I murmured aloud.

The tease had sent a full frontal to me, nude, sexy, legs spread wide. Her pussy glistened like she'd just finished playing too. Slick and ready. All pink and perfect.

Fuck.

She only wrote one sentence: I'm yours if you can get me alone.

Challenge. Fucking. Accepted.

Instant lust filled my brain, and my dick hardened, tenting my jeans. The realization hit me that she did this for two reasons. One, she was fucking horny. I had no problem being the one to satisfy her needs. Two, it was her way of letting me know I finally got my chance. She didn't want to wait any longer. My girl needed me.

I left my room on a mission. There wasn't a soul at The Roost able to steer me away from my goal. Both my mind and my dick were in agreement. I had to locate Rebel as swiftly as possible. I would fucking burst if I wasn't inside her soon.

Hawk tried to talk to me. I brushed him off. Cuckoo stood in front of me, and I growled, shoving him aside as I found Rebel's scent first and her sexy body second. That sweet blossom of a female was bent over a pool table in shorts so tiny her ass cheeks fell out the damn bottom.

She held that stick in her hand, gliding her palm down as I approached. Her pink tongue flicked out of her mouth before she licked her bottom lip. She wiggled her ass as she took her shot and gained the attention of every single guy in the room.

"Mine." The word exploded from my chest like the crack of thunder.

Rebel slowly rose off the table, placing her stick aside. She hopped onto the surface and opened her legs wide. I swear to fuck; I almost punched several of my brothers as they nearly salivated at the sight of those soft parted thighs. She leaned back, giving me a coy smile.

"Say it," I ordered as my voice boomed across the bar.

She didn't have to ask what I wanted. Rebel knew.

"I'm yours, Heron."

Heron's Flame, Devil's Murder MC releases March 2025.

SNEAK PEEK

T HE DESERT WAS A cruel mistress. During the day, she would lead you astray with mirages that promised relief from the cruelty of the sun's heat and constant rays. At night, she ushered in the moon, predators, cool air, and a brisk breeze that robbed your body of warmth. There was no escape. Only miles and miles of no one will ever find you or recover your sun-bleached bones.

As the last of the sun's rays slipped below the horizon, I knew Keys wouldn't see the sunrise. His bike weaved in and out and nearly collided with mine a dozen times. He was barely holding on. It was a testament to the brutality and ruthlessness of the president of the Royal Bastards MC and his will to live. He led with an iron fist. He didn't do shit he wouldn't demand of his own brothers.

We rode for over thirty minutes and out as far as we could until we were forced to stop.

Keys had barely shut off the engine when he fell over and landed with a thud. His normally vibrant green eyes had dulled considerably, and he was beyond the point of pain. A grimace filled his features as he righted himself and leaned against his bike as I managed to climb off my own and ensure the kickstand was down. He didn't need his ride, forcing him to meet death any sooner.

"Never thought I would say this so soon, kid. Raptor was my best friend."

He pressed against his side, and I noticed the heavy trickle of blood that soaked into his t-shirt beneath his cut and stained the fingers of his left hand. He'd lost the leather gloves he typically wore sometime over the last twenty-four hours, courtesy of Scar. "You're a tough son of a bitch, just like your old man was. Raptor would have been proud to see the loyal brother you've become."

Fuck. This sounded like goodbye, and I sure as hell wasn't ready for it.

"Always knew I was grooming you for my position. You're a hard-ass and have what it takes to lead the Royal Bastards. Mammoth and Papa already agree that you're the best choice."

Stunned, I landed on my ass as I sank to the ground.

"I was gonna retire in a few years and name you my replacement. Just feels right. The Royal Bastards are in your blood, son."

Emotion rushed to the surface, and I choked as I tried to reply, succeeding in only saying his name. "Keys." I'd lost my fair share of blood during our mad ride across the desert, and I knew my own hours on this earth were numbered.

Slightly dizzy, I shook my head. "I don't think I'm gonna be far behind you, pres." The words burned my throat on the way out. "I'm a dead man, and the reaper is gonna cash in."

Keys closed his one eye for a few seconds as he struggled to take several deep breaths. The hole where his other eye had been gouged out oozed fluid that glistened in the apathetic moonlight.

"This ain't your last ride, Dex. Devil isn't ready for you yet." He sighed softly. "Gonna miss you. Love ya like you were mine, and that's the fuckin' truth. Took you in, and not a day went by that I regretted it."

Dex. My real name. He rarely said it since we all used road names. The way his voice softened proved he was close to the end. A funny gurgle bubbled up from his gullet, and blood slipped from between his parted lips.

"I love you as much as my old man," I finally whispered, knowing he needed to hear it.

Keys didn't answer, but I knew he had heard. A slight smile lifted the corners of his mouth.

Swallowing hard, I glanced at the moon and watched the clouds passing underneath her strange but luminescent glow. I loved Keys. It wasn't a lie. He welcomed me in and made sure I didn't turn out to be a dumbass. It was hard to hear what he had to say, but I was grateful he did. "I wish—"

The words abruptly ended when I turned back to Keys, and he was no longer breathing. No rise and fall of his chest. No funny sounds. No words of wisdom or promises that didn't mean shit when you were the one left behind.

Tears filled my eyes, and I tried to blink them back, but they slipped down my cheeks anyway. I'd only cried one other time in my life. My old man's funeral. Raptor's death was sudden and shocking. A revenge hit on the club from a rival MC that was taken out before the Scorpions rose up in their place.

Sitting on the sand, I lowered my head and tried to forget the massive sense of loss and the painful ache in my chest that had nothing to do with my injuries. Now that the adrenaline had worn off, I could tell my wounds had reached a critical level.

I'd been too pumped up to notice earlier, but now reality was forcing its way to the forefront. Pain lanced through my thoughts and slashed with brutal clarity.

I thought about the club, my lonely childhood, the hard life I'd grown to love, and all the fucked-up shit with the Scorpions. The last few years of my life had become bloody and ruthless. To be precise, since the moment I joined the Tonopah chapter of the Royal Bastards.

My old man Raptor died when I was only twelve. He'd been a big part of the Royal Bastards and the SAA. I swore that once

I was old enough, I would join the club my father loved and died for. I'd carry on his legacy.

There wasn't any other choice for me. It was my destiny to wear the skull and crown of the club, proudly giving my loyalty to the brotherhood. I'd die for that patch.

Today, I finally would.

I winced, pressing my hand against the wound in my stomach. Acid's blade had gone deep. I could feel my organs through the cut. I'd taken a bullet below my right shoulder that bit like a rattlesnake, sinking with brutal fangs and piercing my flesh.

The pain had been unbearable at first. Now, it was slowly fading. I hardly thought about it anymore, focusing on the heated pulse of agony that probably ripped my intestines apart or shredded some other organ in my abdomen. Blood seeped through my fingers as the swell of the crimson puddle on my shirt grew wider in diameter. I'd forgotten about Acid's favorite little toy.

"Uh," I groaned, scooting along the ground and closer to a large boulder as I fought a wave of fatigue. Every muscle in my body strained with the movement. Dizzy, I overestimated my ability to move adequately, and I nearly knocked over my bike when my leg slammed into the back tire. I'd be pissed if she got a scratch on her. That fuckin' Harley belonged to my father, and I never rode anything else.

The desert air brushed over my skin with a warm caress as night completely descended, but I knew the arriving coolness would soon replace it. The Nevada desert was hot as fuck in the summer, and there wasn't a hint of moisture in the breeze. Kind of like being shot in the face with a blast from a butane torch. It could steal the breath from your lungs. Tumbleweeds rolled on as if to wave at the fool bleeding out in their vicinity. Droplets of blood fed the thirsty sand and hardened the soil beneath where I lay.

Funny how specific memories rose to the surface when you were dying. Like the scent of fresh rain. Pancakes every Saturday morning when I was a kid. My old man's voice was calling my name in a rough tone, always ready to ruffle my hair and ask how my grades were in school.

No one could ever tell me he wasn't a great father. Sure, Raptor did a lot of illegal shit, and over the years, my mother had revealed more than she probably should have known, but he was everything to me back then. When he wasn't on a run, he spent his time at home. He wasn't out whoring around or getting into trouble. My old man played ball with me in the backyard, grilled out burgers and hotdogs, and played his part for my mother. He kept his home, his bike, and his family under his protection at all times.

That was the way shit was supposed to be.

I may have been young, but I'd seen plenty in my twenty years.

And I knew how to take care of my own.

"Lookin' a little uncomfortable down there, handsome."

My head shot up, and I blinked, focusing on the sexy as fuck brunette standing in front of me. Long bare legs led right up to a bikini-clad bombshell with perfect tits and eyes that burned with an eerie crimson flame. "Where did you come from?" How the hell did she find her way out here in the middle of nowhere? "You must be lost, honey."

She smiled a predatory grin that seemed not only strange but hauntingly beautiful. "I know exactly where I am," she replied with confidence. "What's the matter with you? Dying or something?"

Snorting with both irony and humor, I nodded. "I think so."

"You'd be wrong about that, ya know."

When she strutted forward and knelt, her thighs opening wide as she straddled my body, I knew I was a fuckin' goner. My imagination must have been conjuring all kinds of bullshit because her long scarlet nails tapped my chest as she settled over my crotch and rocked her hips as my dick twitched. If I was dying, this was an exciting way to go. I'd fuck a hot chick on my way out.

Why the fuck not?

I thought that as she leaned in nice and slow until our faces were only a couple of inches apart. A wicked grin hovered on her lips until it vanished so fast that I didn't have time to blink between what happened next.

Her entire face transformed into the scariest fucking thing I'd ever seen. A skeletal visage appeared and snarled, the bones covered in ligaments and a light layer of muscle in sporadic spots that twisted her features into a nightmare.

"Fuck!" I shouted and shoved her back, cracking the back of my head against a boulder as I tried to scramble away. "What the fuck are you!?" I demanded, wincing at the pain in my skull.

Shit.

I must be going to hell because this was nothing less than the freakiest monster I'd ever seen, and I liked horror movies.

The face disappeared, and so did the brunette. The tall form of a man replaced her. He stood in an impeccably clean black designer suit, perfectly pressed and crisp. His closely-shaven face and features were something you would see in magazines.

Too perfect to be real.

Black hair was slicked into the latest style, falling into one of his eyes in that carelessly attractive way most women adored.

Coal-black eyes stared back at my perusal, but the flash of crimson confirmed he was the same creature I'd been staring at a few seconds prior. This man and the woman were the *same*—two completely different appearances of one demented being.

"I think you're beginning to understand now," the deep voice answered my thoughts. "In case you doubt my identity, I thought it necessary to show you two of my favorite forms."

His identity? "Huh?" It wasn't my most articulate moment.

"We don't have a lot of time, kid. You're gonna die soon." He shrugged, slipping his hands into the pockets of his trousers. "I can offer you a different life."

My eyes widened at his words.

"A bargain."

"Why?" I asked. That was the first thought in my head. Why me?

"Let's just say I prefer to approach those who have what it takes to further my own personal agenda. Humans intrigue me. The ruthless and sadistic the most. Like attracts like, after all," he added with a light chuckle, "Eternity is *so* boring."

Blinking, I finally figured out who he was—the *goddamn devil*. Holy shit!

He appeared amused. "I knew you were smart enough to catch on. The question is, did you like the little stunt I pulled? Interested in a little payback for your enemies?" He sauntered forward and opened his arms wide. "Want to stick around and ensure those that harm your loved ones and club get what they deserve?"

He knew my answer was yes, but I didn't say it aloud.

"There's no guarantee the Scorpions will ever receive punishment. Want Keys' death to matter?" He hooked a thumb over his shoulder. "Or is he gonna die without meaning? For a club that couldn't give two shits, they killed a man as important as your dad?"

Fuck, the devil was good at his presentation.

"I can give you what you need. Want to scare them? Rip them apart? Send their souls to hell for eternal torment?" His eyes gleamed a brighter red with the prospect. "Because I like fucking with sick and demented souls."

A grin widened my lips. "Fuck yeah." But I wasn't interested in turning into a woman. Fuck that.

The devil chuckled. "You won't be getting that handy little trick. I must keep some of my abilities mine alone."

Yeah, I figured as much.

"What I can do is give you a gift that few can boast." He tilted his head to the side. "You familiar with the Grim Reaper? What he does?"

Yep. "Like killing people with a scythe?"

He smirked. "You could say that. A true reaper harvests souls. He sends them to hell for eternity. It's the soul that matters." He knelt before me, careful not to get a speck of dust or sand on his suit.

"For you, I'll throw in a little something special. Auras are the true reflection of the soul. You want to know who's worthy of the Reaper's blade? The darkest souls. Those covered in ebony shadow."

My head grew a little fuzzy with his description. The blood loss was starting to take its toll.

Two fingers snapped in front of my face. "You don't have a lot of time left, Dexter Lanford. The devil is knocking. Will you answer?"

I groaned as the pain in my body increased. It was a trick. I knew that.

The devil was messing with my head, but I also knew I wanted retribution and blood for what the Scorpions had done to my club.

Keys and Lockjaw were dead. That shit wasn't going unpunished even if I had to come back from the dead to do it.

The devil laughed and stood, snapping his fingers once more as a piece of parchment appeared out of thin air. An invisible pen began writing words in onyx ink quickly down the page, leaving two blank lines at the bottom. He lifted his other hand and bit off the edge of his finger as blood dripped from the digit, and he signed the bottom line in his dark crimson blood. The wound healed immediately.

"Your turn."

He thrust the contract close enough that I could read the contents from top to bottom. A twisted smile curved my lips. I was bound to the individual who signed this contract. Lucifer Morningstar.

Given carte blanche, my only requirement was reaping souls and handing them to the devil to fulfill the contract. No specific number was written down, but explicit instructions for recognizing souls that were to be reaped.

If I failed to take out those marked, I'd violate his contract. Punishment could mean revocation of my abilities and immediate death. If that happened, my soul was Lucifer's. Either way, he won.

Brilliant. There was no way to trick the devil. He was a master of deception and had already proved it. Lucifer was ensuring he received exactly what he wanted. If I didn't sign his contract, he would simply find another soul that would. It wasn't complicated to understand.

"My club?" I asked, taking an unsteady breath.

"You will take the position that Keys wanted. The president of the Royal Bastards MC. The devil's instrument." He paused and leaned forward, touching the tip of his finger to my forehead.

A shock jolted my body back into full awareness, and I realized I had nearly died before I could sign the contract. "Shit," I cursed.

"You will take on a new road name. A name that personifies your position and authority, and you will rule over all others beneath you. Your brethren will also join and sign my contract. Each member will take the Devil's Ride. If they live, they'll become patched in. If not, they are not worthy."

"Yes," I finally agreed, swiping a finger through the blood on my abdomen and signing the blank line on the contract.

At the devil's urging, I took on a new identity to cement my leadership and allegiance to my club.

It wasn't hard to come up with a road name that instantly evoked fear. A name that perfectly described my transformation. I wanted vengeance, the suffering of my enemies, and the calculating ability to rain down hell upon those who deserved it. A name that symbolized the cold, hard bastard I'd become.

Grim, the Reaper.

Lucifer's hand pressed to my chest, and he smiled with triumph.

"Reap. Your. Souls."

My body was seized in a wave of pain so strong that I felt every limb ripped apart all at once. A cry of agony left my lips, and my eyes fluttered shut. Convulsions rippled across my thick frame. Inhuman wails echoed and bounced off the rock, joining my own in a macabre cadence that was some demented form of celebration. I briefly wondered if it was all a lie and I'd never awaken again.

Too late.

My soul was bargained and sold.

The devil owned Dexter Lanford, the Grim Reaper.

Devil's Ride, **Royal Bastards MC** is available now.

ABOUT THE AUTHOR

Nikki Landis is a romance enthusiast, tea addict, and book hoarder. She's the USA Today Bestselling Author of over seventy novels, including her widely popular Tonopah, NV RBMC series. She writes wickedly fierce, spicy romances featuring dirty talkin' bikers, deadly, possessive reapers, wild bad boys, and the feisty, independent women they love. Nikki loves to write character-driven, emotionally raw stories where protective, morally gray anti-heroes fall hard for their ride-or-die. She's a mom to six sons, two of whom are Marines. Books are her favorite escape.

She lives in Ohio with her husband, boys, and a little Yorkie who really runs the whole house.

Made in the USA
Las Vegas, NV
15 November 2024

11822824R00097